KIDNAP

KIDNAP

Philip McCutchan

Hodder & Stoughton
LONDON SYDNEY AUCKLAND

British Library Cataloguing in Publication Data
McCutchan, Philip
  Kidnap.
  I. Title
  823.914 [F]

ISBN 0-340-58237-5

Published by Hodder and Stoughton,
a division of Hodder and Stoughton Ltd,
Mill Road, Dunton Green, Sevenoaks, Kent TN13 2YA
Editorial Office: 47 Bedford Square, London WC1B 3DP

Typeset by Hewer Text Composition Services, Edinburgh
Printed in Great Britain by Biddles Ltd,
Guildford and King's Lynn.

KIDNAP

ONE

Mr Blundy sat behind the wheel, shoulders hunched forward, knuckles white from a ferocious grip, eyes staring, mouth tight. His wife Ag sat in the front beside him, ready with words of advice. Mr Blundy didn't dislike driving, but he was more of a potterer and this abortion of a road scared him stiff, made him fancy he was on the circuit – odd, for a potterer, he sometimes thought, to be crazy about motor racing – at Brands Hatch or Silverstone. There were definite similarities: no traffic lights, no pedestrian crossings, no intersections, but plenty of fast-moving vehicles. *Zoom-zoom-zoom* they went, *roar-roar*, going much faster than he was. Even the exit roads looked rather like the slip road into the pits. Yes, there were similarities all right, and Mr Blundy would rather have been looking down from one of the bridges, like from a stand. It seemed like one bridge after another, did the M1, vantage points from which vandals could drop heavy weights on innocent motorists.

Innocent, eh.

Bloody likely! With what was in the boot?

Mr Blundy gave a quick sideways glance at Ag, sitting there like a mountain – the old Granada could just about cope with her weight. Only just: she acted almost like an anchor each time the car started.

Ag didn't seem at all worried, but she saw the glance. "Keep your eyes on the road, do," she said.

"All right, all right, keep your wool on."

"No call to be rude, there isn't. Look at that man."

7

"What man?"

"In that car, just look! Doing ninety, I'll be bound. Should be more police – " She broke off, sharp. "Shouldn't have said that."

No, she damn well shouldn't. Mr Blundy felt his stomach fall away, felt the sweat soak into his clothing all over; the wheel was slippery from his hands, too. Suddenly he remembered one of his old dad's sayings: you couldn't hide anything from God. God, Dad used to say quite often, was everywhere, looking and judging and noting down. You never got away with anything, not with God, who was the ultimate Old Bill. And God knew very well what was in the Granada's boot. Mr Blundy had a sudden and disturbing vision of God sitting there, on the Armco barrier, judging and noting. Mind, He'd had plenty to note down in the past.

Oddly enough it had all had its origins, Mr Blundy ruminated with bitterness as he drove north to the remote wildness of the Yorkshire Dales, in that night – months and months ago now – when Ag had insisted on his going straight and had thus struck deep into his independence. At the time he'd just come out again, after a longish time over the wall. . . .

Ag had one of her moods on. Blundy was sitting in the big, shabby armchair in front of the electric fire – it had been a rotten summer – a bowl fire he'd picked up cheap years ago in the Portobello Road. He felt sunk almost without trace in the chair's vastness, all except for his skinny legs that were resting on the other chair, equally big and shabby and shapeless, temporarily vacated by his ever-loving wife while she prepared supper: kippers, by the smell . . . Mr Blundy's nose twitched but his eyes were on the china pig that stood on the mantelpiece above the fire's golden-metallic glow. He studied the pig with real affection: he loved Piggy, even though Piggy was fat like Ag. Piggy had the snub nose common to pigs, china or otherwise; it also had large eyelashes painted chocolate brown, a number of blue spots overlaid with black and green stars and a blue oblong strip on either flank inscribed with the words "Premium Bonds", and a slit in the top for reception of coin. Mr Blundy had

8

never won a prize in the draw because he had never in fact bought any Bonds; the pig was emptied from time to time so Mr Blundy could go down the boozer. He didn't blame the pig; he loved the pig for its own sake, because it looked friendly, because it looked happy, because it didn't look as though it wanted to kick him around. He had bought it on holiday years ago in Southend and thereafter it had joined all the other nick-nacks in the small, stuffy parlour – from Margate, Clacton, Great Yarmouth and the Portobello Road – now overlaid with dust and the smell of cooking.

That night, apropos the pig, he heard Ag's accusing voice right across the years, right along the miles of railway line and pavement between Southend and Bass Street, Paddington.

"Shocking waste of money I call it."

"Fifty pence."

"Could have had a meal or two on that."

"Well, I bought the pig instead, didn't I."

"Just plain selfish, that's you all over."

Hell, Mr Blundy thought, back in Bass Street, which was at least more comfortable than the Scrubs, never supposed to spend a penny on myself, am I. Bitter thoughts filled his mind, gave his long, narrow face a look of sorrowful helplessness.

Removing his gaze from the pig, he sniffed the kitchen aroma again.

Kippers.

He'd have loved some nice salmon.

He'd have loved to have been born rich. The shabby chair – so big that it had been dead cheap when he'd bought it from a junk shop, for people these days seemed to prefer chairs that looked like lavatory seats – creaked under the thought-impulses of wealth. Mr Blundy, ill-nourished looking and beaten as he was by life and by Ag, had plenty of big ideas. A nice big house somewhere, a mansion standing in its own grounds – somewhere posh like Golders Green, with a garage housing a Rolls Royce. Meals in expensive restaurants, good clothes from Austin Reed, a whole collection of china pigs, Wedgwood if they made them. Fat cigars and bugger the health lark. Many other things, unlimited beer being one. But money didn't come that easy, not even when you were self-employed on crime. From all you read in the newspapers, lousy lot of liars, you'd think fifty-quid notes grew on every bush just waiting to be nicked by all the villains the police never caught. *Unsolved crime rate rising*, they kept on saying in the papers. To Mr Blundy, not long out of prison after being copped on a handbag-snatch job, the law seemed only too well on top of their trade: his personal unsolved-crime rate had fallen cruelly, he was the living proof of the newspapers' mendacity. All the same, there was cachet in the self-employment angle, real class; it was great not to have a boss and a clocking-on machine and to take a day off whenever you felt like it, Ag permitting, of course. Ag was the fly in the ointment: you couldn't give in your notice to Ag. On the other hand, Ag was also security: you didn't get the sack.

Mr Blundy knew all about the sack.

Van driver, house painter, steward on a coaster, night-watchman, street cleaner, washer-up in hotels, you name it, Mr Blundy in his pre-self-employment days had been sacked from it. Lazy, they said, the swine – inefficient, thick, couldn't be trusted. Bird-brained, unable to keep his mind on the job. It was true he couldn't do that, certainly; his dreams kept on getting in the way, those dreams of *bigness*, of being somebody. Every profession he'd ever taken up, he'd seen himself at the top with astonishing clarity: Blundy's Transport (van driver), Blundy the Builders (house painter), Captain Blundy (steward on the coaster), Sir Ernest Blundy (Barclays Bank, where he'd nightwatched), Mr Blundy, Head of Council Services (street cleaner), Mr Blundy the Managing Director (washer-up). What with all that to think about, there hadn't been much time left for work, not really. During his periods inside, however, he hadn't seen himself as the prison governor; loyal to his self-employed status, he'd been a Kray, of a sort – Big Blundy. Don't get in my way, not unless you want to be duffed up. King of Crime – that's me. Even the screws jump to it when I say.

But now the reality: "Come and get it, then."

Ag's voice. Mr Blundy called back that he was coming, belched emptily, sighed towards the china pig and hoisted his skinny body from the chair, an arm of which moved sideways as he did so, spilling sawdust.

10

He went into the kitchen, that place of grease and dirty saucepans and dishes and the gas stove as black as night and Ag's big bum looming at him as she bent over the stove, an overfed ham. Mr Blundy felt an intolerable ache somewhere in his vitals. Was it any wonder he had other problems as well as lack of cash? Out of bed or in it, Ag was a dead loss. Sex tormented Mr Blundy as a result, really tormented him. For Mr Blundy, no sex symbol himself, London had never swung. Not even right back in the sixties, when he'd been young.

"There you are, then," Ag said briefly, slapping a kipper on a cold, cracked plate. "Eat your fill."

Munch, and pick the bleeding bones out of your teeth. After supper, the business attack.

"You got to go straight again."

"Eh?"

"You heard. Since you come out this time, you brought nothing home, just sweet *nothing*. Right?" Ag speared a pickled onion on a fork, thrusting it down to follow a hunk of mousetrap cheese long past its sell-by date and thus bought cheap. "Lucky I saved a bit. But the kitty's empty now."

"But Ag, I – "

"Empty, I said, didn't I?" Ag's lips folded in behind the pickled onion. "I say it again: empty."

"I don't want to go straight."

"It's not what *you* want."

"Look, Ag, there's no *money* in it. Anyway, I can't go straight, go back to all that, is it likely, is it bloody *reasonable*? Just ask yourself."

"I have. I've answered myself, too. It'll be difficult for you – "

"Difficult? Jesus Christ!" Mr Blundy threw up his hands at a blatant understatement.

"Don't blaspheme. I won't have blasphemy. I won't have your prison talk."

"That's just it, isn't it?" Mr Blundy said. "Prison. Who'd give me a job, I'd like to know?" He'd found a formula, or he thought he had, but it didn't work.

Ag gave a jeering laugh. "No, you wouldn't know. That's you all over, Ern. Thick as two planks. And bone idle with it." She changed her tack, her big red face grim and ugly.

11

"All right, then. Don't get a job. Don't go straight. Stay in crime. *But do something*. Get some cash. Got any ideas?"

"Well . . . not just at the moment like." Mr Blundy paused, ran a hand through his thinning hair, thinking. "Tell you what. I'll have a word with the boys. Down the boozer."

"What d'you mean, down the boozer?"

"What I said. Down the boozer."

"All right, all right, bloody parrot talking. Come into money, have you?"

"Don't be daft. Give me five quid, eh, Ag?"

She hooted.

"You have to spend money," Mr Blundy said, coming out with one of his acquired tenets, "so's to *make* money. Stands to reason, does that."

"Your money. Not mine."

"No money," Mr Blundy said firmly, "no boozer. No boozer, no talk with the boys. No talk with the boys, no jobs. No jobs, no money. Full circle – just like that." He waved a hand in the air, grand and powerful, the tycoon, the chairman of the board tossing off a business axiom at the AGM, but Ag was no shareholder.

"Get stuffed, then," she said.

She had him in a cleft stick. She wouldn't part with a penny – she still wanted him to go straight really. Of course he could always nip down the boozer and have half a pint, he could manage that, but then he wouldn't be able to buy a round and he'd look a right mean so-and-so. Besides, the boys mightn't be there, which would be a waste of money since he couldn't just glance in and go out again. That would look odd, all things considered. These, of course, were just excuses to himself – he knew that. The real reason he didn't go was that Ag always knocked the stuffing out of him by withdrawing her moral support. Silly bitch, she'd approved his going into crime in the first place, now she was going to nag him out of it again. And she would win, no doubt about that, no doubt at all. Mr Blundy sagged down into his chair, looking as worn as the chair did. Maybe he'd see the boys some other time.

Or maybe he wouldn't. Bugger Ag.

* * *

"There's a good job in the *Standard*," Ag said next evening.

"Oh, yes?"

"Oh, yes." She threw the paper at him. "Don't sound so upset. Got to do something, haven't you?"

Mr Blundy sighed. "What's the job, then?"

"Contract cleaning. People's homes."

"Don't be stupid, Ag."

She glared. "Why stupid, stupid?"

"Me with my record?"

"You on again about being in prison? Don't have to wave your crime sheet, do you? You can deal with that and you know it."

He blinked at her. "How?"

"How, he asks. Use your brains, if you have any. Just you get a fake card or whatsit. Under a new name. Those pals of yours, they'll fix you up. Pay them out of your wages. When you get them."

"Oh, yes? And what, may I ask, about bloody income tax – PAYE?"

Ag rejected the income tax excuse as beneath contempt. "That lot! Never even catch up with a cold. You got to be sharp, that's all. And Social Security's just as overworked, which is their word for bone idle. Like you." She could never resist a personal dig. "Get away with it easy, you know you will."

"No, I don't."

"Then all I can say is, you'd better find out. I've had enough." She got up, stood over him, hands on hips, voice as shrill and hostile as a factory hooter. "Sitting around on your backside all day while *I* go out cleaning, aren't you ashamed of yourself, Ernest Blundy? What my mum and dad would have thought, not that they ever reckoned much to you anyway . . ."

On and on and on.

Mr Blundy's head whirled, making him feel sick. The bitch. He did his best, didn't he? He felt close to tears. Why he'd ever married her . . . But he knew the answer to that: pregnant, she'd made herself out to be, and that was a laugh all on its own – they'd scarcely done it since. Ag didn't like sex. As for her mum and dad, well, least said the better.

Mum, long since in Highgate Cemetery and good riddance, had been SuperAg; poor Dad, incinerated at Golders Green because it was cheaper, had been a kind of Mr Blundy – talk about history repeating itself. The trouble was, Ag's family had been craftsmen, a cut above the common working classes – Dad Gaotcher had been a watchmaker in Highgate – so Ag had sunk in the world the moment Mr Blundy had dropped, after marriage and via the sack, from a more or less responsible position in the stores department of a main dealer and distributor in the motor trade (Lord Blundy of British Leyland, Champion Exporter) to a van driver. Not that Ag could look down on his family – and didn't, credit where credit was due. She looked down only on Ernest Montgomery Blundy. Mr Blundy's father had been a tradesman in his own right, a master stonemason, graves and that. A very superior man, and largely the fount of Mr Blundy's high ideas. The fount also of Mr Blundy's inability to date to make any headway against life: Dad had been too bloody perfect, right in all he did, bung full of self-confidence, convinced that the watching eye of God could find no fault anywhere. By contrast, nothing had ever gone right for Mr Blundy. As a child even his toys had never worked as they should. Dad had seen the bright side of that, too: it was good for the character to face adversity and to do without.

There had been too bloody much of doing without, more and more as the significance of his jobs had dwindled. Well, it was a fact of life: some people went up, others went down. As his dad would have said, there wasn't room for everybody at the top.

No fairness.

Mr Blundy examined the Situations Vacant, mutinously.

The advert said to apply to Mr Nostrage at Cook's Contract Cleaners, and at nine-thirty the next day Mr Blundy applied and was dead unlucky. It was true that massive unemployment had at last hit London and the south, but house cleaning was not all that popular. Everyone was too grand to be a skivvy now. Mr Blundy got the job, or one of them since four persons were required. On a temporary basis, probably a tax and insurance fiddle: Mr Blundy was not asked for P45s or anything like that.

"Quite a good choice," Mr Nostrage reported later to his superiors. "Name of Smith, Ernest Smith . . . been self-employed as a painter and decorator, so he's used to visiting good-class homes. Not much on top, but that doesn't signify. Dreary to look at, but he's polite and, well, obsequious, I suppose you'd say, which is what the customers want. I'll start him Monday."

Up bright and early on Monday morning and out into a dirty, wet London day. Soggy trousers and the usual dearth of bloody buses, Mr Blundy dived into the Tube, cursing Ag. Cook's Contract Cleaning wasn't going to provide the cream, barely the skimmed milk really. Ag was so short-sighted, never took in the full extent of his dreams. Big Blundy . . . and lovely young girls with not much on – and that soon to come off – fighting for his favours in that lovely big mansion where he sat smoking a cigar and dressed in a silk dressing-gown like Noël Coward, deciding which of the girls he wanted that night.

Just as well Ag *didn't* know that part.

Anyway: ultimately he would have to go back to where the real money lay, only next time it would be the big stuff. Oh yes – definitely.

TWO

"Well, how was it?"

"Rotten. Bloody rotten."

"That's right. Moan, moan."

"I'm not moaning. I'm just stating a fact, that's all. I don't like the bloody job."

Ag shrugged and went off to the kitchen. Mr Blundy heard her banging saucepans about in a temper. Gloom settled like a pall, a thick blanket of despondency. Mr Blundy's back ached from unaccustomed work, hard work with broom and hoover, polishing cloths and all that. Women's work, and his workmates were mostly women – not personable women, not birds. Hags, more like, middle-age and up. Very different from the unclad young girls of Mr Blundy's dreams.

Sod the job.

Down the boozer on Saturday evening, spending what Ag allowed him out of his own hard-earned wages. A nice pint of mother-in-law – stout and bitter. Froth edged Mr Blundy's greedily sucking mouth. A finger dug him hard in the small of the back, causing some spillage.

Mr Blundy swung round indignantly. Indignation didn't last; this was a piece of luck. An old friend.

"Just come out, Ern," the friend said.

"Heard you was inside."

"Yes." The speaker was not unlike Mr Blundy, but taller; thin and slightly stooped with an overlarge head that was

16

totally bald in front and covered at the back, when last at large, with shoulder-length brown hair. This was now trimmed to prison requirements. It would grow again. The man was Bernie Harris, known as the Loop in Mr Blundy's circle, the reason for this name having been lost in the mists of time in both senses of the word, though there was possibly some connection with his extraordinarily hooked nose, which looked quite like a teapot handle. Bernie Harris, whose perpetual grin, friendly or oily according to taste, hid a crafty and dangerous mind, had been in and out of prison since the age of around twenty, and Borstal before that. He was unique among criminals in that he changed his line after every nicking, on the principle, quite a clever one, that the Old Bill expected all villains to stick to their last. This stratagem hadn't in fact helped all that much, but the Loop clung to it obstinately. Versatile, he was: safe-breaker, con man, forger, pick-pocket, car thief . . . you name it. Not very successful, never having served a proper apprenticeship in any skill. Jack of all trades. As a safe-breaker he'd been pathetic, waited so long for his charge to go off on his one and only attempt that he'd been a sitting duck for the Bill.

"So what are you doing now?" Mr Blundy enquired.

"This and that. How about sitting down for a natter? I'll take a pint with me, thanks very much."

They carried their glasses over to a table in a quiet corner for the natter. The Loop asked, "How's things with you, eh?"

"So so."

A quick glance and a nod. "Not so good, eh? What you been doing, Ern?"

"Going straight," Mr Blundy said reluctantly.

"You never."

"Got a job."

"Jeez!"

"Bloody house cleaner, aren't I?"

"Well, blow me down, what a lark." The Loop considered for a moment then asked, "How's the wife?"

"She's okay."

"That's good."

"Yes."

"How's she taking it, Ern? You going straight. I mean, there's not a lot of money in going straight, now is there?"

"There bloody isn't." A lot of feeling had gone into that utterance. "But as a matter of fact it was Mrs Blundy that insisted I *should* go straight."

"You being serious, Ern?"

"Yes." Mr Blundy lifted a hand and scratched moodily at his head. "Maybe she'll get over it. Me, I reckon she will. She likes being in the money, does Mrs Blundy. So do I."

The Loop nodded. "Time of life," he said.

"Eh?"

"Mrs Blundy. Menopause. Made her go funny?"

"She had that a few years back. Or said she did." Mr Blundy suspected that Ag had used it as an excuse to stop doing it for a while, but the while had gone on and on. The Loop was frowning in what looked like concentration, his mind not quite with Mr Blundy. Mr Blundy fell silent too, moodily contemplating his emptying glass and wondering if the Loop was going to refill it for him. Then the Loop piped up again.

"Whereabouts is your house-cleaning job?" he asked.

"South Ken."

"Class, eh. Decent houses."

"Money," Mr Blundy said. "Oodles of it. Pours out of their lug-'oles. Never seen the like, never."

"Right," the Loop said. "Worth bearing in mind, is that. "You've got the *entrée* – or will have once they know you. And trust you, like." He paused. "Got a bloke to see. Be seeing you – maybe put some business your way."

The Loop went off then, not buying his round, which was just like him. Bloke to see, Mr Blundy thought, my arse! He didn't put much hope in the Loop's unspecified offer. On the other hand, well, you never could tell. In any case, nothing ever did come of it.

It wasn't him – house cleaning. It was demeaning. It was murder. Backache, dust up the nostrils, cheeky kids. After the following Monday's gruelling work Mr Blundy went into a caff for a cup of coffee as the mean bitch at his workplace hadn't given him one.

18

He felt people were staring at him, looking at failure.

"You all right, love?" A small, skinny old waitress with a shrivelled face. Mr Blundy looked blank and said, "Me? Yes, I'm all right. Thanks for asking." Deep down he longed for some conversation, longed to open up to someone who wasn't Ag, tell them his troubles, his hopes and aspirations – tell them he wasn't all right at all. "Nice of you. Not many bother these days."

"That's all right, love, if you're all right you'll want the bill."

So that was all she'd wanted, to know whether or not to bring another cup of coffee, or a bun. She shoved a bit of paper at him and moved on. Mr Blundy got up and paid at the desk then went out into the street. Raining again, sod it.

Mr Blundy didn't so much as mention the possibility of work via the Loop's good offices. Not to Ag; for one thing, Ag didn't much like the Loop. Bernie Harris, she'd said more than once in the past, scorning the use of his nickname, was a twister. Well, of course, that was dead true, he was; but she didn't mean it quite like that. She meant that even his pals couldn't trust him. That might also be true, though Mr Blundy couldn't say the Loop had ever done *him* dirt.

Anyway, it wasn't fair. Life wasn't fair. It just wasn't fair at all. All those shop windows, trudging as he did along Kensington High Street. Big stores, little boutiques, they were all there for people who had the sponduliks. Expensive clothes, wonderful eats – delicatessens full of cheese and caviare and that – gift shops with lovely things made of leather and whatnot. Girls going in and out. Mr Blundy liked today's fashions, they accentuated the curves and crevices – those crevices! – wonderfully, even if it was a bit difficult sometimes to tell if it was a bird or a fellow till you got round to the front and looked back. The hair and bums were mostly unisex.

Ag didn't have crevices. Not that he'd noticed.

On the way home after work that evening Mr Blundy called in at the usual boozer. He had hopes of a word with the Loop, but the Loop wasn't there. Mr Blundy went home to Ag more bitter than ever. He was going to give up the job if the Loop didn't come up with something soon. The DSS was a far better prospect.

Saturday, and they went to Brands Hatch. There was to be Formula 3000 racing, not the big stuff like at Silverstone, but still. Ag didn't like motor racing anyway, so why take her at all? Mr Blundy knew why: she insisted on coming, wouldn't let him out of her sight in case he picked up a bird. Ag moaned all the way there, criticising his driving, criticising the poor old Granada, which had certainly seen much better days.

"We'll never get there."

"Yes we will."

"If we do, we won't get home. Going to fall to bits, if you ask me."

"No it isn't."

"Don't look after it proper, that's the trouble."

Mr Blundy ground his teeth. All that polishing, all that sweat, all the muck when he changed the oil, all the hard work and skill when he buried his head beneath the bonnet. All he said was, "She'll do." What he wanted was to give Ag a good, hard kick up the backside . . . a reflex action made him ram the clutch out involuntarily. There was a surging jerk as he let it back in, bang.

"Your driving! Want lessons, you do."

"Shut up, do."

An indrawn breath. "Don't you ever tell me to shut up! I never heard the like, never." She shook with anger. So did Mr Blundy, being at the end of his tether. He had his revenge. He got her in a real tizzy by the time they made Brands, by using his feet in conjunction with his loaf. She thanked God for a safe arrival. "In spite of your rotten driving," she almost spat at him.

They entered the car park for the enclosure – Mr Blundy certainly couldn't afford the stands. It would be a day of trudging from one vantage point to another in order to snatch the best views of the track, but it would also be a day of thrills and a display of authoritative knowledge on the part of Mr Blundy. He would come into his element. He would participate in, and communicate to Ag, each and every

20

emotion suffered by the drivers as they went into Druids or stormed along Bottom Straight to zoom, howl and snarl their thunderous passage round South Bank Bend and past Clearways for Pilgrim's Drop and Hawthorns.

"Come on, Ag." Once parked, Mr Blundy was impatient for the smell of oil and burned-up tyres.

"Coming, aren't I? Don't fuss." Ag came out bum first, dragging a basket of lunch – paste sandwiches, bottles of lemonade, packets of crisps. She handed all this to Mr Blundy, who locked the car doors meticulously, knowing his cloth only too well. They made their way over rough ground, all tufts of grass and hard-packed earth ridges where mud had been churned up and then dried. Down to the roadway running behind the stands, under the Dunlop arch. Ag went into the Ladies', leaving Mr Blundy to wait with the lunch basket. Mr Blundy cast an eye towards a bar farther along; he could do with a can of lager. Fill up while Ag emptied: past experience told him there should be ample time.

In the bar, a miracle happened. The Loop, ahead of him in the queue, whistling softly to himself and waving a ten quid note all ready to place his order. No time like the present: Mr Blundy left the queue and approached the Loop.

"Well, blow me down if it isn't Ern."

"Didn't know you liked motor racing."

No comment from the Loop on that, but a curious look in his face. "How's things, Ern?"

"Same." Mr Blundy lowered his voice. "Hoped to be seeing you down the boozer."

"What about, Ern?"

"What you said. Maybe a job."

"Oh, that." The Loop gave him a dirty look. "Do you mind? There's a time and a place for everything. Right?"

"Sorry, mate. Sorry to offend, like."

"Yes, well." The Loop looked mollified. "Now listen, Ern. I might be able to . . . help. See? No promises. I just might. Doing anything Monday night?"

"No – "

"See you in the boozer, six-thirty." The Loop turned away. Mr Blundy left the bar. Outside, Ag was waiting, glaring round and about.

"That was quick," he said.

"What was quick?"

"What you went to do, pee. Usually take – "

"Place was all locked up, wasn't it?"

"Oh."

"And I s'pose you went for a drink."

"Yes, I – "

"With that friend of yours. Don't tell me, I know. I just seen something I don't like: Bernie Harris."

"Oh, yes?"

"What's he want?"

"Oh . . . nothing. Ag – "

"Don't you act the innocent with me, Ernest Blundy. Just tell me what he's after."

She'd have to know sooner or later. "Just might be able to put something in my way, like."

"Such as what?"

"Didn't say. Come on, Ag. Let's get along to the pad-dock."

"Paddock," she said disparagingly. "Silly name for a garridge. Don't know why I come." (But *he* did.) "Now look, Ern. That Bernie Harris. You watch your step. Put everything he says under the microscope."

"Yes, I will, Ag. I haven't committed myself to any-thing – "

"Then don't you, ever." She was quite angry. "All he does, it's for his own benefit, see."

"Yes, Ag. Let's get to the paddock before it fills up. Wait outside if you like. It's cheaper."

"You shut your face."

In the paddock, the busy mechanics were at work on last-minute adjustments. Lovely cars – great gleaming monsters of speed to Mr Blundy, though Ag remarked crushingly, as she always did, that she was surprised how small they were close to.

"Telly gives you the wrong impression," she said.

Mr Blundy's mind wandered to Silverstone and the Grand Prix the year before. The Formula Ones had all been there – Ferrari, Lotus, Williams – in their shining immaculate

22

cellulose, all colours of the rainbow. Mr Blundy had got close to Nigel Mansell, his current God – had even managed to touch his splendid overalls, which was really *great* and made Mr Blundy go all hot and cold and shiny eyed. Gerhard Berger had smiled in his direction but Mr Blundy, humble as ever, had turned swiftly and seen the bird who responded to that smile. In Alain Prost's stall, or cubicle, or garridge, Mr Blundy had acquired a spurt of engine oil on his anorak, and even though it wasn't Nigel Mansell's engine oil, it was great too – Mr Blundy would treasure that black stain all his life: Alain Prost's Uniflo, how big an accolade could you get, it was dead lucky was that, better than seagull shit even! Today, leaving the Brands paddock after a whole hour's lovely ramble, Mr Blundy and Ag turned left.

"Where we going?" Ag asked.

"Druids. Best view there."

"Best view of crashes."

Mr Blundy set his teeth. Bitch. Druids was certainly a nasty sharp corner and a lot of drivers did spin off there. People like Ag had a way of saying motor-racing fans only went for the spin-offs and the brew-ups, for the thrills of injury or death, but it just was not true of the real fan. Not true at all: the real fan appreciated the skill in cornering, the mastery of the gearbox, the use of the brake and the rev counter – not the bad luck or slight misjudgment that led to accidents. The real fan hated seeing a noted name go wrong and was as sincerely sorry, when that happened, as any soft-hearted old lady in lace and lavender over the death of a cat. Ag wouldn't have that, though. When Mr Blundy remonstrated she squashed him with a scornful laugh.

Ag, however, had her physical uses at Brands. By now the place was filling up tight and the common enclosure crowds were, like Mr Blundy and Ag, sorting themselves out towards the best vantage points, a situation in which the tank-like qualities of Ag made their passage a whole lot easier. Ag simply moved forward and Mr Blundy followed, into and through a dedicated crowd of men and women, men and women mostly bearing transistors and little boards to which were clipped lap records, some with stopwatches, some with banjos, many with a mass of beer cans and baskets of sandwiches and flasks of coffee wedged down with Dad's pullover. And a variety of dress, or in some cases undress: half-bare girls (lovely), men with funny hats or baseball hats or no hats at all – hairy men, smooth men, sometimes smelly men. It was great, and it wasn't much like Ascot. Mr Blundy fancied he'd be right in saying the Queen hadn't yet come to Brands. He wondered she didn't, really.

Afterwards, it took Mr Blundy all of two hours of stop-start-stop to get clear of the car park.

"Why come when you got to go through all this after?"

"It's a day out and I enjoy it."

"Always got to be what *you* enjoy."

"You can always get out and walk."

"No need to be rude. Or stupid."

"Leave off, can't you."

Argue, argue. Argue all the way home to Paddington. Mr Blundy's head swelled and retracted and swayed. He thought maybe he ought to have his blood pressure checked some time, though he doubted there was anything the quack could do so long as Ag was still around.

Monday evening, no Loop in the boozer.

Every night that week Mr Blundy went down the boozer at six-thirty, feeling that perhaps he'd gone and mistaken the day, though he was sure he hadn't.

No Loop.

Mr Blundy made a few casual enquiries, very discreet: the Loop hadn't been in at all. Not all week.

All week!

That week stretched for months.

Through the rest of the year, September, October . . . over Christmas, over New Year.

Into February. Mr Blundy tried to forget that wonderful but evidently phony promise, but it rankled: it wasn't fair, to raise his hopes and then just vanish into thin air (and not inside; Mr Blundy had checked that one out). It was all part and parcel of his lot, just another thing that hadn't come off, another thing that had gone wrong. From time to time the image of his father flashed

24

before him, saying: "It's good for you to go without, Ernie lad." God, hadn't he gone without enough yet?

You couldn't do anything else but go without, not on the DSS. Over Christmas Mr Blundy had gone down with 'flu and had felt so ill after that he'd chucked the house cleaning.

Then the Loop turned up.

Down the boozer, Saturday night, first week of February – that was when the miracle happened. The Loop breezed in bright and happy, with just a casual apology.

"Been busy. This and that – getting things organised. All for you, Ern, all for you. Takes time to organise a job like this one." The Loop clapped Mr Blundy on the shoulder, hard. "Bring your glass over. We'll talk."

Over once again to the nice quiet corner – quiet in a special sense, though really it wouldn't have mattered where they talked considering the din. Bloody juke-boxes, Mr Blundy thought angrily as he was cannoned into one off a fat girl and lost half his stout-and-bitter.

"This is big," the Loop said. They were having to talk ear-to-mouth through the din.

"Screw job?"

"No."

There was a pause.

"Well, go on," Mr Blundy said. "That's if you want to. I mean, if you want me in on it."

The Loop looked him over shrewdly. "I do, Ern. If you're up to it. Like I said – it's big."

"How big?"

"Very, very big. Real money this time. *Real* money."

Mr Blundy, feeling a curious stir in his vitals, nodded. "Go on," he said again.

The Loop looked over his shoulder, all very cloak-and-dagger now. He said, "P'raps better not here, eh. Let's go for a walk, all right?"

"All right." Mr Blundy drained his glass and got to his feet. He followed the Loop out of the boozer and away from Bass Street. The Loop led the way south, down towards Praed Street and Paddington railway station. He talked after a while, quietly, without seeming to move his lips.

"I reckon I can trust you, Ern."

" 'Course you can."

"Wouldn't have asked you else."

"No."

"So that's all right. Now, I told you this was big. It is. So just a word of warning, Ern, a word to the wise." A hand gripped Mr Blundy's arm, very hard. "Once you're in, you're in, right."

"Yes."

"No backsliding."

"No."

"Any backsliding, any grassing – *anything* I don't like, see – you could be in dead lumber."

"Oh."

"Not could be. *Will* be. Just a word of warning, that's all. I know it's not really necessary, Ern."

"No." Mr Blundy felt a shaft of fear, like ice forming on his spine. He hadn't liked the Loop's tone; the Loop was putting in the steel. The boot could follow. The Loop, benign look, half-bald head, hook nose and all, could be very dangerous. In the past, Mr Blundy had heard about the results of the Loop not liking people. Nasty. Now was the time for Mr Blundy to get out if he was going to: if he didn't, his chance was gone, his number would be at risk of being up thereafter – it would be too late once the Loop started talking. But he ws being offered a chance and it might be a last chance. God knew, he hadn't got far in forty-odd years. To get on you had to take risks; the higher you aimed, the bigger the risks – stood to reason, did that.

Wealth, real riches? All those lovely shops in Kensington High Street, the mansion with the swimming pool, the girls competing for his favours. Big Blundy. Butler, footmen, chauffeur for the Rolls.

He couldn't chicken out now. Simply couldn't. Though such had been the menace in the Loop's tone that half of Mr Blundy rather wanted to. Duffings-up, burial in hard-core destined for motorway construction, concrete blocks secured to legs to keep a body anchored on the bed of the Thames, that sort of thing. But that didn't have to happen. Not if he played his part and didn't grass.

"Want to hear more, do you?"

"Yes." Against his better judgment? God, he didn't know what his judgment was any more. Only one thing was sure now: that low, half-strangled "yes" was his committal.

"Right," the Loop said. "You're in, Ern." He picked at his nose. "Bin on me mind a long while, this has. Bin working up to it like. Matter of fact . . . it's why I went to Brands that time."

"Brands?"

"Getting the feel of it, like. As of now," he added, "I can't say how much is in it for us. That depends, see. But whatever it is, your cut, Ernie boy, will be a guaranteed fifty per cent."

Mr Blundy was astonished. "Fifty! That's generous, that really is generous, Bernie."

The Loop spoke modestly. "Full partnership, Ern. Share all, rewards and risks. Eh?"

Mr Blundy was doing sums. Fifty per cent? And a big job. Could be thousands . . .

"What's the job?"

"Kidnap."

THREE

"That's what I bloody *asked* him," Mr Blundy said impatiently. "Why me? I asked. Because you've got a big car already so you won't need to nick one for the job, he said. And because you know Brands, he said. And because you've got Ag, he said, and Ag can help you mind the kid. And no other attachments, no dependants . . ."

"Kid," Ag said. "Who is this kid?"

"Don't know yet, Bernie didn't say. But Bernie . . . you wouldn't think so, p'raps, but Bernie's soft on little kids. He don't want him hurt or neglected. That's where you come in, Ag."

"Oh. Is it?"

"Yes. And there's another thing. Another qualification I got."

"And what's that?"

"You and me, we're mobile. Or can be when needed. Specially since I chucked up work, see. You can leave yours easy." Mr Blundy paused, eyeing the china pig on the mantelpiece, willing it to bring him luck. "More important to Bernie, though, is your Aunt Ethel."

Ag stared. "How does she come into it?"

Mr Blundy hedged. "Time we went to see the old lady."

"You've never called her that before."

"Well, never mind what I've called her before, Ag. Point is, she's got the cottage up in Yorkshire – "

"Meaning we take the kid up there?"

Mr Blundy nodded. "Quick of you, that was, Ag. Up

28

there in the Dales, all remote, like, and inaccessible, you can disappear for a while. As long as it takes like. Bernie, he wants to get the kid right away from the London area, right away, fast as he can after he's been lifted. While he does the negotiating with the parents. And your Aunt Ethel, she – "

"She's not daft, you know. Not daft at all. Or senile either. What do we – " Ag broke off. "How old's this kid, did Bernie say?"

"Thirteen."

"Ah yes, thirteen. So do we say, like, we've just had a thirteen-year-old son?" She laughed shrilly. "Come to that, what does the kid say to Aunt Ethel? Eh?"

"What he's told to say," Mr Blundy answered irritably. "Now look, Ag. Your Aunt Ethel, no, she's not daft. She's not senile. But she's as deaf as a bleeding post, the old bag. *And* blind as a bleeding bat without her specs. Also, she's independent, which is just as well, seeing there aren't any neighbours within a couple of miles . . . oh, she's wonderful, I'll not deny that, doing for herself and all. But – "

"She's not immobile either. The moment she goes out of the house she'll be on to the police. You'll never persuade her the kid's there because he wants to be."

"But she won't know – "

"And she's not too blind to read the papers."

"She won't bloody go out," Mr Blundy explained in a shout, "because we won't let her, see? We'll do the shopping and that – "

"Keep her prisoner?"

"Just for a bit, yes. Not prisoner exactly. Just look after her, see to her for her own good, at her age she needs that. Just till Bernie's got his end fixed, that's all. Soon as he's ready he lets us know."

Ag glowered. "It's a stupid scheme," she said scornfully. "What happens after – about Aunt Ethel, I mean? Once we've gone, she blows the lot, doesn't she? Or do we pay her to keep her mouth shut? Not that she would."

Mr Blundy shook his head. "No, Ag. We just don't let her *see* the kid. That's all. Keep him hidden. We won't be there all that long. Live in the boot, p'raps. Or a cowshed."

Ag shifted about in the overstuffed chair. "Well, I dunno. I still say it's a daft scheme. Just like that Bernie Harris."

"It's something new for him, Ag."

"All the more reason something'll go wrong. He told the truth in one respect, though: kidnapping's big. Too big. Why, we'd go over the wall for years and years! I don't know about you. You're used to it. But *I* don't want to go inside." She aimed a finger at him. "I'm having no part in this and nor are you. You just tell that Bernie Harris I said so!"

Mr Blundy broke out into a heavy sweat. "I can't, Ag."

"Can't, eh. What do you mean, can't? Got a tongue in your head."

"Well, I *can*, of course. But then again I can't. Don't you realise what'll happen? Look. The Loop, he's told me the facts, hasn't he? He's trusted me with the info. So if I back out, or if you do, then what happens, eh?"

"You tell me."

"We get duffed up," Mr Blundy said.

"Duffed up?"

"Me and you, Ag. Duffed up very, very bad. Razors – the lot. You don't want that."

Ag's face went redder than usual. She gasped, began to pant. "Oh God," she said. "Oh God. What you gone and got us into now, you – you *stupid*, rotten, useless . . ."

Her voice tailed off. Then, to Mr Blundy's immense astonishment, she burst into tears. He really didn't know what to do. Never had she cried before, not in all his memory. It was terrible; it was like the Tower of London falling over. Mr Blundy blew his nose in embarrassment, reached out and patted Ag's heaving, wrestler-like shoulder. "There, there," he said. "Don't cry, Ag. Don't fret. I'll think of some way."

She sobbed, and between the sobs she spoke. "You're not capable. You've never been any use. Sack, nick, sack, nick. Oh God have mercy on me."

Mr Blundy blew out his breath in despair. He tried again. "Now look, Ag, be – "

"Shut up."

"But I don't want to – "

"Just shut up, that's all."

Mr Blundy shook with fear, fear of the Loop and the Loop's tame thugs. Being duffed up . . . He'd seen it happen inside, never mind the screws, it had been quite appalling. Kicks, blows, knives, tender parts assaulted nastily, even things inserted where they had no business to be, sharp things. Duff up a shade too much and you *killed*. The Loop had never killed, to Mr Blundy's knowledge, but there had been a suggestion before they'd parted that the Loop might leave any revenge to his mates. There was no knowing what those mates might have done in the past.

Mr Blundy had no appetite that evening, but, feeling tenderness was called for now, he got the supper. Tin of sardines. Then bed.

In bed, Ag was just the usual lump but tonight a lump that cried. The lump hadn't even wanted the light switched off, in case the duffers-up came, having got the word by telepathy presumably. Mr Blundy was at his wits' end: without Ag's co-operation he could never pull this job off anyway, duffers-up or no duffers-up.

Or could he?

No, said further reflection, he couldn't. All sorts of reasons why not: you needed two to keep a constant watch on any kid, kidnapee or not. Besides, Ag would never let him go off on his own, not all the way to Yorkshire . . .

No, she wouldn't, would she! Just the mere threat of it – oh, brilliant! God be praised, he'd got it in one.

Mr Blundy prodded the lump. "Ag . . ."

"For God's sake shut up."

"Thought of something, Ag. I don't like to see you upset like." He spoke tenderly. "I don't really. Same time, I don't want to be duffed up. Nor you neither."

No response, but he believed she was listening.

"Go on me own." Oh, she'd never wear that! "Don't you fret."

The lump turned, heaved over was more like it. "You'd never."

"If it saved you – "

"How daft can you get. Wouldn't have a hope. Besides, don't care about me, do you?"

"Ag, I said, it's because of you – "

"Never *think*, do you? That Bernie Harris, he'd know you told me it all. I'd be a danger to him, wouldn't I? Could yack, couldn't I? Don't you see? I'd get done while you're away."

"Sort of . . . silenced like?" There was a gleam in Mr Blundy's eye. Genuinely, he'd not thought of that. But it was quite a good point in support of his crafty plan. "I don't reckon Bernie would do you on your own – "

"Wouldn't chance it."

The lump was obviously agitated now. Mr Blundy said, "Well, it's a risk, of course, that I'll not deny. I dunno, Ag. It's a bit of a mess . . . you reacting like this."

"Oh yes, of course, blame me." The lump turned back the other way, withdrawing bedclothes. "Blame me for not wanting the razors."

"Oh, Ag, I don't blame you at all," Mr Blundy said in a considerate tone. "I always knew this was risky. But do think on the bright side, Ag. Pull this job off and it'll make all the difference, all the difference in the world. There'll be thousands in it for us. You and me. The Loop won't be going for chickenfeed on this, is it likely? We'll have a new car, Jag if you want. Nice big house in the country, butler, skivvies . . ." Big Blundy. Big Blundy went on, laying it on thick. Plenty over to invest for their old age. No more going out to work. Don't want to end your days as a char, Ag. All the clothes you want, and all those expensive restaurants. Better than a tin of sardines. And no duffing up.

A cautious query from the lump: "What about the kid?"

"He'll be all right. He'll go back to his mum . . . when Dad pays up."

"I've always liked kids."

Mr Blundy gave a jerk. "*Have* you? First I heard of it."

"Well, I do. It's sex I think is so dirty."

"World'd come to an end without it. Even reverends do it."

"Perhaps they do." She heaved again, in Mr Blundy's direction this time. "How much do *you* reckon's in it?"

Mr Blundy recognised the note of greed. He said casually, "For us, our fifty cut? Dunno. I told you – "

"Make a guess."

"Two hundred thousand nicker," Mr Blundy said at random.

There was something like a whistle. Mr Blundy hazarded another guess: he reckoned he'd got there.

Next morning, relieved and expectant, filled with optimism for a lovely rosy future, but with butterflies in the pit of his stomach all the same, Mr Blundy made his way to a telephone kiosk at Victoria Station. A long way to go, but the Loop had been insistent: from now on, full cloak-and-dagger.

Just a brief call. "Hullo. It's me."

"Uh-huh."

"All okay. Ready when you are."

"Fine. I'll be in touch. Just wait."

Click.

FOUR

Days passed, bowel-gripping days, before there was another contact, another very late-night and clandestine meeting, with the Loop. Though he did his best to conceal it both from Ag and the Loop, fear had seized Mr Blundy in the interval. *Was* it going to be so dead easy? The Loop had seemed confident enough, but then he always had at the start of anything new. His optimism and confidence had always lasted to the point where he was nicked and went over the wall, after which he came out smiling again and full of fresh plans, formulated whilst inside. The Loop, oddly perhaps, was the sort who made friends and over the years he had learned a lot from them.

This time his confidence was boundless. Nothing could go wrong; it was all very well based.

He told Mr Blundy the details of the kidnapee.

"Name of Barnwell," he said. "Harold Barnwell. Nice, well-mannered kid. Goes to a posh boarding school. In Kent, it is. His old man's a millionaire a few times over. Made it in scrap iron and that. Bloody great mansion in Herts. Haverstock House."

"Going to be lifted from there, is he? Or school?"

"Neither. Kid's mad keen on motor racing – "

"So that's why you – "

"Yes. Nips out and goes to Brands whenever there's anything on – plays truant like, if it's termtime. The job'll be done at Brands, see, date yet to be notified. It'll be dead easy . . . and the old man's the sort who'll pay up pronto,

34

without ever risking so much as a wink to the Bill. Done me homework, Ern . . . Dad's barmy about the kid, and so stinking rich the money don't signify."

Mr Blundy licked his lips. "How much?" he enquired.

"Try a million to start with," the Loop said. He had some questions to ask Mr Blundy, picking Mr Blundy's brain very closely about Brands Hatch, its security, its grounds, its official set-up. Mr Blundy, tendering his advice with a fan's enthusiasm, had an idea the Loop was merely confirming what he'd found out already. If so, very wise, Mr Blundy thought. And his share would come to half a million. It was quite staggering. Maybe two Rollses. Maybe two butlers.

The following morning Mr Blundy put some speed behind Ag.

"Best get your Aunt Ethel fixed up, Ag. Write today, eh?"

"Think about it."

"No point in delaying, Ag."

"Not got the date yet, have you?"

"Well – no. But it won't be long. Be an idea to soften the old girl up in advance, eh? Prepare her, like, why not?"

"Don't need it," Ag said briefly. "Don't have no visitors. Be only too glad to have us."

"You sure?" Mr Blundy margarined some toast, that and a cup of tea being breakfast. In a few weeks' time it would be caviare or something, in a silver dish.

" 'Course. Must be lonely for her."

"Some folks like being on their own."

Ag didn't bother to respond. After Mr Blundy had finished breakfast, she got herself ready to go off to her job as charlady. "Come on, then," she said. "What you sitting about for?"

Mr Blundy sighed, got to his feet and went into the kitchen to wash up. His mind flew ahead of the washing-up bowl to Brands Hatch. The Loop had said it wouldn't be long. The washing-up done and in all conscience that didn't take long either, Mr Blundy sat and rested for a while with a cigarette; then he thought he'd go for a walk, a long one since it was a nice day and he needed to have his time occupied till the off.

35

He went down Bass Street and crossed Praed Street, going south for Hyde Park. He crossed the Bayswater Road and entered the comparative peace of the park. He liked its greenery, all that grass and the trees, a real oasis. London's traffic roar diminished a little. It was early and there were not many people about, just the odd park keeper and cop. There was a slight mist hanging over the trees and kind of spreading the sunlight behind it so that instead of a bright sun there was a sort of golden haze.

Lovely.

Mr Blundy breathed deep and walked on. He went right across the park till he came to the posh side, Knightsbridge. And Rotten Row. There were some riders, birds mostly, good-lookers too. Not that Mr Blundy liked people on horses: they looked and acted too superior, always staring down their noses at the horseless population. Some of those birds would be a sight better for a good roll in the hay – and Mr Blundy had a bet with himself that they wouldn't look so high and mighty with their feet on the ground instead of in the stirrups. Like the Household Cavalry, over there in Knightsbridge Barracks, shiny-topped tin soldiers who looked sort of forlorn when off their horses, silly way their boot-tops flapped when they walked, you could see the shoddiness. Mr Blundy paused to give a V-sign towards the back of a young bird who was probably a duke's daughter, mounted on a jet-black horse. Lot of snobs.

But things were due for a change. Mr Blundy was about to join the nobs – and wouldn't he love that!

Him on a horse.

Ag on a horse.

Mr Blundy laughed aloud. Stone the crows – Ag on a horse!

She'd look right daft, would Ag.

Have to be a shire horse.

A real old-fashioned brewer's dray puller . . . and she'd look like Queen Elizabeth the First riding down to Tilbury to yack at the dockers about her having a woman's body but a man's heart, or whatever it was she said. Whatever it was, it didn't really tie in with Ag. Horse's body perhaps . . . Mr Blundy had read some history but not much.

36

On a golden dream of the future, firmly thrusting down his fears since worry didn't help, Mr Blundy moved towards the Kensington Gardens end of the park.

The Round Pond.

Kids – young kids, not yet snobs.

Little boats with sails or engines, out-thrust by eager young hands. Shouts of delight, or dismay when the boat stopped in mid-pond. Sunshine and laughter, and a handful of nannies with plush, custom-built prams. White kids and not-white kids . . . this was Embassy territory and there was tax-free money around. Or Customs-free. Or something. Never mind. Mr Blundy felt bitter about it though, thinking of what *he* had to pay on his fags and beer.

But kids were kids.

Not their fault that Dad fiddled.

Mr Blundy sat on a bench, warmed himself in the sun and looked at kids. Bloody Ag. He wouldn't have minded a kid. Nice to have a son to follow on, a daughter to spoil and fuss over. He was going to feel right sorry for Harold Barnwell's dad – but of course the bugger had only himself to blame, getting so stinking rich, you asked for it really, condemned the kid to kidnap from the cradle onwards. Mr Blundy ruminated on young Harold. Of course you couldn't expect a kid to get fond of his kidnappers, stood to reason, but Mr Blundy would do his best to come to an understanding during the time the boy was in his charge. He sounded like he had the right ideas – playing truant from that posh, smarmy school. Maybe he rebelled against all the snobbery – after all, his old man had come up from the gutter. The kid may have seen through the shams of society.

Motor-racing fan, too.

Probably supported Nigel Mansell.

Treat him right and he could be great to have around. After all, the money wouldn't be any skin off of *his* nose. It would all be a bit of a lark to him once he knew he wasn't going to be duffed up, hurt in any way at all. Just a question, really, of getting his confidence . . .

A ball, coming with some velocity, struck Mr Blundy on the nose. "Bugger," he said. "Little bastard."

He clasped his nose, then looked at his hand. By some

37

miracle, no blood. But it had hurt. A small boy stood off at a distance, warily.

"This your ball, son?"

"Yes." The boy giggled suddenly and Mr Blundy frowned. Perishing little nob. Very expensive-looking T-shirt and shorts and shoes. Posh. Dad in the Diplomatic most likely. Mr Blundy, not feeling diplomatic, spoke again.

"Hit me on the sodding nose it did."

"Yes, I know. I'm awf'lly sorry."

God. How did these foreign kids do it? The boy looked like he might be an Arab, or a Turk or something. It was the schools, of course, the private schools. Mr Blundy wiped his face with a rather dirty handkerchief. Here was he, Ernest Montgomery bloody Blundy, more than forty years English, and he could never produce that perfect, precise, classy English accent, never in a thousand years.

"Here," he said. He threw the ball.

The small boy caught it expertly. "Thanks very much. I'm awf'lly sorry to be such a nuisance."

Mr Blundy waved a gracious hand. " 'S'all right, son."

"Is your nose all right?"

"It'll live."

"I'll go, then. Goodbye."

"Bye-bye, son."

The boy turned and ran away daintily, bouncing his ball. Mr Blundy gave a moody grunt. All right for some. Mr Blundy watched the olive-skinned figure run round the pond towards Kensington Palace and vanish. He got up from his bench and went towards the water, reaching it just as tragedy struck a miniature power boat about six or seven feet from the edge.

There was a sound like a brass band out of tune as a small boy, white this time, burst into tears. As this happened, a tall, skinny woman with no boobs rose from another bench and hastened to the scene.

"Oh, dear. What's happened, Master Timmy? Poor Master Timmy." Master Timmy, eh.

"It's stopped. It's not going to – to come back, Nanny." The wails increased.

"Oh, poor Master Timmy," the tall woman said again. She

38

dithered, caught Mr Blundy's eye. Mr Blundy looked away. None of his business, was it, and the woman was no bird. "I daresay it'll come back soon, Master Timmy dear." She had a brainwave. "Throw a stone in behind it and the ripples will send it back, like little waves, Master Timmy."

"You throw it."

"All right, Master Timmy." She did. It was spot on; the boat sank, plop, gurgle.

The small figure danced with rage. "*Bugger* you."

"*Master Timmy!*"

The din was now appalling. The small red face was like a squashed plum, spurting in all directions. "Can't the man help?" the plum demanded, pointing a finger at Mr Blundy.

Mr Blundy wondered why the flaming hell he hadn't buggered off fast.

"Oh. Well." The skinny woman looked helplessly towards Mr Blundy. "I wonder if – I wonder if you'd be so terribly kind . . . ?"

Silently, Mr Blundy cursed. Wet feet were wet feet and drenched trousers were uncomfortable. But he was going to have to get accustomed to kids. Call it practice in the interest of the job. The Loop would like that, showing keenness and dedication. He glared round wildly, seeing trees. "I'll get a stick or such," he said. "Branch, like."

"Oh, would you? That's terribly kind, thank you so much."

Mr Blundy went into action, stared at with hope. The yells stopped: the man was going to make it all right. By sheer luck Mr Blundy found a branch, half dead, hanging off a tree and within his reach. Seizing this he wrenched and twisted and pulled. Not that dead . . . but it came away suddenly, almost sending him flat on his back. He carried it to the scene of the sinking and grubbed about with it in the spot indicated by the small boy. After about a quarter of an hour he brought in a gumboot and when the thing emptied itself it disgorged a contraceptive device. The tall woman bent to examine it but was beaten to it by the small boy.

"Balloon, Nanny."

"No it isn't, Master Timmy."

"Can I have it?"

"No. How disgusting."

Mr Blundy kicked his haul back in and started again.

Success: after another ten minutes the boat was beached.

"Oh, thank you *so* much. You've no idea . . . Master Timmy treasures that boat. It's terribly good of you to spare the time." She turned to the child. "Say thank you to the – the gentleman, Master Timmy."

"Thank you. Here." A dirty paper packet was brought out from a pocket and a sweet was extracted by grubby, pond-watery fingers that had touched the supposed balloon. "Have this. It's my last but one."

The tone had been a little grudging. Mr Blundy said, "That's all right, son."

"Don't you want it?"

"No – yes, I mean. But I don't want to take your sweets, sonny – "

"All right, then." The sweet was popped into the mouth. Big blue eyes stared at Mr Blundy. "Thanks awf'lly all the same. It was jolly decent of you. I'll tell my father how kind you were. So'll Nanny, I expect."

"Well, thanks," Mr Blundy said, marvelling at juvenile upper-class assurance: the words had come oddly in such a piping little voice. "What's your dad, then – one of the ambassadors, like?"

There was almost a sniff. "Good gracious, no. My father's a duke. I'm a marquess really, only Father won't let the servants use my title in case I get big-headed. Goodbye."

The noble back was turned. Nanny smiled dismissingly. Mr Blundy walked away, back towards the Bayswater Road and Bass Street, Paddington.

Cor.

A brush with the aristocracy, just wait till he told Ag! They were still there, all right, if you looked hard, even today. Not a bad little cuss, but Mr Blundy was glad he hadn't wet his feet. Just for that bloody boat. The ducal castle was probably stuffed full of them, boats and other toys bursting out all over, tidied each night by the footman. Not that Mr Blundy hadn't felt a little glow at being thanked, and so nicely too, by a nob. Twice in one short morning – ball and boat. It was not often anyone thanked Mr Blundy. It was nice, that little glow of virtue. Kids were nice, too. Genuine. Saw things clear, like. No nonsense. To kids, Mr Blundy was a man, not a worm. He would do his best to make real mates with Harold Barnwell, give him as good a time as possible. He would owe him that much in any case, seeing as he was going to be the means to the lolly.

Besides, if anything went wrong, it might count with the Bill. Kind of insurance, really.

Action, a day or two later, came nearer.

Mr Blundy and the Loop were walking along the Edgware Road, heading north. The work-out, the Loop said, was going well.

"Going to give me the details, like?"

"Such as concerns your part, Ern – sure. Mine so far as it crosses yours. You and me, we do the actual snatch together. And Mrs Blundy."

"*Ag?*"

"Yes. Kid'll be set at ease by a woman."

"By Ag?" Mr Blundy sounded doubtful about that. "You'd best explain," he said, looking bewildered.

"Right, I will. Me, I'll be dressed the part. Be in genuine race-meeting gear . . . T-shirt with the insignia of a whatsit, pit marshal – "

"Genuine? You can't buy – "

"Not buy, no. Got it from a pal, didn't I? Just listen, Ern. Right from an early hour, I'll be near the paddock entrance, see? The kid, he never misses out on a visit to the paddock and I – "

"How d'you know he'll be at Brands? Haven't thought of that, have we?" Mr Blundy was alarmed: fall at the first fence?

The Loop was far from worried. "Didn't need to. Not special thought, like. Kid *always* goes to Brands when anything's on, I told you that before. This time, well, it's only Formula 3000, but it's a Championship race – plus there's a special thing for anyone who likes motor racing." The Loop paused. "Blimey, you should know. I'm fixing it for when the old champs have promised to be in the paddock: Jackie Stewart – "

41

"Emerson Fittipaldi – "

"Jackie Ickx – "

"Mario Andretti – "

"Chris Amon, Scheckter – "

"Stirling Moss. 'Course I knew that," Mr Blundy said. He gave a whistle. "So that's the day, is it?"

"Yes, and mind you keep your mind on the job. The kid. Don't go all moon-eyed about them champs, right?"

Mr Blundy gave a slow nod, his thoughts at Brands Hatch. All those names . . . of course anybody who loved the smell of motor racing, the tang of excitement, wouldn't fail to be there on that special day. All the same, there could be a snag and Mr Blundy voiced it. "That kid. Okay, so he'll go for the names, sure he will. But what if his teachers stop him? Eh? If he's like played truant before – "

"No worries. This is the permissive society, Ern. Teachers has changed, see. Probably take a back-hander."

"Teachers, take a – "

"Teachers is the same as anybody else, and they're paid peanuts or so they moan. Don't worry about it, Ern. Harold wants to go to Brands, they don't let him, he shoots off just the same. Now they do let him. Saves trouble all round. Right?"

Mr Blundy nodded.

"I told you, didn't I, I've taken a lot of trouble to get all this right." The Loop looked around. "Come on, let's cross over here, by the lights. Go back the other way."

They crossed. The Loop continued, as they walked south again, "Spent time and money on it, researching."

" 'Course."

"He'll be there, all right. We tail him from the paddock. Kid don't go for the stands. Watches from the enclosures, so he moves around, sees the races from different angles. And there's all those wooded parts, right?"

Again Mr Blundy nodded. He and the Loop had discussed those wooded parts in detail. They were thick, they were secluded, they were largely barred to the public but they were easy of access just the same, and they were strategically sited for the Loop's purpose. As the pair went on walking, seeming so innocent, the Loop expounded and Mr Blundy listened in a certain awe to his effrontery; and in growing alarm also. There seemed to have been a lot of organisation going on without his being party to it, though obviously his advice, judicially given, had been properly heeded. An ambulance and its crew, all in the Loop's pay – not Red Cross or St John's, those incorruptibles, but got up to look like St John's – were part of the set-up. Mr Blundy's own car was to be parked good and early, not in any of the Brands' car parks but in Farningham, a couple or so miles from the circuit.

"Make sure the Granada's fit for the job, eh?" the Loop said. "Proper garridge overhaul. None of your DIY. No expenses spared, right?"

"Talking of expense," Mr Blundy said, "this ambulance. Reckon you won't have fixed that cheap. Whose share does it come out of?"

"Both."

"Oh."

"When I said fifty per cent, I meant fifty per cent of the net. Not the gross."

"Oh."

"Out of a million nicker, Ern, the expenses'll be chicken feed."

"Well – yes. What's the ambulance for?"

"Put the kid in."

"How? I mean, how do we get him in? I mean, he's not sick." Mr Blundy ticked over, or thought he did. "Has an accident, like, does he?"

The Loop chuckled."No. He'll be dealt with hypo-dermically, see."

At this point Mr Blundy felt like passing out himself; but was positively assured by the Loop that the injected fluid would be harmless in a long-term sense, being intended only to render the recipient quiescent and compliant for some hours – for long enough, in fact, for the Granada to reach Yorkshire.

"Granada, eh."

"Yes."

"Not the ambulance?"

"Not the ambulance, no. Ambulance is only to get him past the gate at Brands. In Farningham he transfers to your

43

car. By that time he'll be what I said, quiescent. No trouble in the back and later on, when you find a quiet spot, you can transfer him to the boot. Kid's small for his age – fit nicely. Bring blankets and a nice soft eiderdown, and pillows. And rope. Just in case like. Precaution – that's all."

"Who's going to use this hypodermic, Bernie?"

"You are, mate."

"Oh, Christ, no!" Mr Blundy felt the onset of panic. "Not me! I can't use them things!"

"Easy – can't miss." The Loop had such boundless confidence. "Me, I can't be spared just then. I'll be bringing up the ambulance, see." He added, "Ever been in hospital – had an anaesthetic?"

"No."

"Oh well. Before the actual anaesthetic," the Loop explained, "they give you what they call a pre-med. Makes you all dopey like so you stop worrying about the sawbones. Everything's fine, know what I mean. Needle in the bum, the fleshy part. Can't miss that, now can you, eh?"

"Miss what?"

"The bum."

"No, I s'pose not, Bernie. But I don't like this, I don't mind telling you – "

"You'll have to like it, mate, you're committed now." The Loop's voice had hardened. "Remember? You don't want no trouble from the boys. And the kid'll be absolutely okay, just sleepy, that's all. But get yourself a gag along with the rope, all right? Just in case, like I said."

The Loop reached into a pocket and brought out a package which he thrust into Mr Blundy's hand.

"What's this?"

"The needle, and two phials of the dope. Full printed instructions within."

"Oh my God." Mr Blundy hastily concealed the package. He didn't like it but he certainly didn't want trouble from the boys. But there was a point that had been nagging at him. He said, "That ambulance. Said it would look like St John's, didn't you?"

"That's right, Ern."

"What about the real crew? I mean, the one that'll be in

44

attendance, like? Won't they think it funny, having another crew there?"

"No," the Loop said. "By that time they won't be thinking anything."

"You mean – "

"Forget it, Ern. Not your business." The Loop wouldn't say any more. But Mr Blundy felt cold all over: kidnap was one thing and was dangerous enough. But murder – if that was what the Loop was suggesting – was another. But there were the boys . . . and perhaps it wasn't murder. Perhaps the St John's crew would just be waylaid and kept somewhere until the thing was over. Kept by the boys probably, very secure.

Below Mr Blundy's accommodation lived a Mrs Whale; Mrs Whale was on the phone and was willing to take messages. She had taken one when Mr Blundy got home. The message was reported to him by Ag, who was looking worried.

"Snag," she said. "Fly in the ointment."

"What?"

"Aunt Ethel. Phoned, she did."

"Aunt Ethel did? She never! She's not on the phone, Ag. Never known her get on the blower."

"Not Aunt Ethel. Why don't you listen. District nurse in Windersett. Didn't know, the nurse didn't, Aunt Ethel had any next-of-kin. Not till now."

Mr Blundy sat down in the big armchair, his head in a whirl what with one thing and another. He asked, "What's this all about, Ag?"

"Aunt Ethel," Ag said patiently, "has been in 'ospital. Come out six weeks ago and bin creating. All on her own, like. Except the nurse goes in."

"What's she been in hospital for?"

"Partial Gas-ter-rectumy."

"Eh? Gas-ter-what? Gas-ter-rectumy did you say, Ag? Mean farting? She's been farting too much?"

"No, I don't mean farting, you – "

"Other way round, then. *Gas-ter-rectumy.*" It had a rolling sound to it, and Mr Blundy rolled it round his tongue. "Air up her bum, sort of air enema?"

45

"Don't be daft, Ernest Blundy, nor vulgar neither. I asked Mrs Whale. Said the old lady's had part of her stomach removed."

"Don't sound like it." Mr Blundy shook his head in some perplexity. "Gas-ter-rectumy, eh. These quacks, they don't half come up with some names, Ag. Sounds like that vet programme on telly, when the vet shoves his arm up – "

"That's enough of that, thank you. Aunt Ethel isn't a cow and never mind that you've called her that before now. This throws a spanner in the works, don't it?" Ag said shrilly. "There'll be quacks and nurses all over the show, won't there? Fat chance of taking a kid up there and keeping him hidden!"

"Oh my God." Mr Blundy put his head in his hands and made a moaning sound, almost a keening sound. The Loop positively could not be let down, put off till Aunt Ethel had no further need of medical care. The whole thing was set up and the timetable couldn't be altered for a whatsit. Aunt Ethel, gas up the bum or not, was an integral part of the work-out. Mr Blundy reminded Ag about the duffers-up. He urged her, having just had a brilliant thought himself, to look on the bright side.

"Just the right excuse for us to go up there, Ag. Look after the old girl in her hour of need, like. Till her stomach's back."

"It won't *come* back. Don't be daft. Stomach doesn't come back after you've had a – what Mrs Whale said."

"All right, Ag, it won't come back. We stay, like, till she's better, that's all. It gives the whole visit a reason, see?"

"And that kid stays silent right the way through? And Aunt Ethel doesn't even know he's there . . . screeching and bawling his head off 'stead of keeping quiet, I'll be bound."

Mr Blundy told her about the hypodermic.

Ag didn't like it any more than Mr Blundy did.

"I don't like that," she said.

"Bernie said it's perfectly safe." Mr Blundy told her about pre-meds.

"Pre-meds is all very well, Ernest Blundy. Pre-meds my foot. In hospital you're not usually bound and gagged after. Or held to ransom. Makes a difference."

"Well, I don't know. As a matter of fact you *are* sort of bound. Them surgeons, they pounce on you, hold you down so you can't duff up the bloke with the knife. Reflexes, see." Mr Blundy mopped at his face; he was terribly agitated. "Look, it'll be *all right*. The Loop, he doesn't want to harm the kid any more than we do, stands to reason, he's got to collect the money, hasn't he, and you don't – "

"When does he do that? Collect the money?"

"He'll let me know more later." Mr Blundy mopped again at his face. "This hypodermic, now. Goes in the backside. Easy, the Loop said . . . but I dunno about easy. Not without practice, like."

"Backside's big enough," Ag said briefly.

"Not a kid's. Anyway, the instructions say, in a muscle." Mr Blundy frowned and looked dubious. "Thing is, Ag . . ."

"What?"

"Ought to practise. You got to probe around for a muscle, shouldn't wonder. Can't have things go wrong, can we? Kill the poor little sod for want of practice. We can't risk a balls-up, Ag."

"Practice, eh."

"That's right. Like Aunt Ethel's surgeon . . . before he give her that gas-ter-rectumy."

"Oh, shut up, do." Ag paused, glaring. "Practice on what?"

"Why, the yuman body, Ag."

"*Whose* yuman body?"

"Well, now." Mr Blundy pursed his lips.

Ag jumped on what she took as Mr Blundy's unspoken suggestion. "Come off it. I'm not green. I know what you're screwing yourself up to, or trying to, and you're not practising on me and that's flat. Anyway – wouldn't help to knock *me* out for the count, would it?"

"No need to use actual dope, Ag."

"No dope?" She paused, hands on hips. "Oh. You mean just probe, like?"

He nodded. "Just probe, Ag."

Her big face suffused. She seemed about to have a stroke. "Then you can just probe off!" she shouted.

* * *

47

That night Mr Blundy lay sleepless in bed with a load of cotton-wool strapped to his backside with much plaster. Ag had announced that *she* would give the kid the needle and she too had a need of practice, not wishing to commit murder. Ag's aim had not been good; Mr Blundy doubted if she had been cruel on purpose; she was just naturally ham-fisted. As she jabbed and withdrew, reread the instructions and jabbed again, Mr Blundy set his teeth and thought of the future. Thought of wealth. That big house, the gravelled drive, the sweep before the porticoed porch, the butler waiting with a silver salver, ready to open the door of the Rolls, silk swimming trunks borne by a footman for the master's dip in the heated swimming pool, gold-bottomed. The birds who would be waiting for him when he emerged. (Ag didn't seem to figure in these thoughts.) Lovely – but this was an undignified route to gracious living. He sweated. Phew! Why hadn't he married a nurse? Probe, wrench. God, why couldn't the silly cow get there?

It was murder.

Bum like a pin-cushion . . .

At least, since with any luck Ag's skill might have improved by the time it was needed, that poor kid wouldn't need to suffer like this.

But all things come to an end, of course.

At last, Ag gave a shout of triumph, leaving the needle, however, *in situ*. Mr Blundy felt a curious dragging sensation in his fleshy part, closely followed by slight pressure as the body of the water-filled hypodermic syringe drooped down upon his buttocks.

"Finished?" he asked shakily.

"Think so."

"Pull the bloody needle out, then."

"All right, all right, just checking what it says."

"Oh, God."

D-Day was the Sunday, and Sunday was nice and bright: sunshine, little white-flecked clouds streaking across a blue sky before a light wind. Fresh and invigorating, a lovely day for the visiting champions, parading before the admiring fans in the full splendour of their overalls, which were artistically

48

daubed here and there with engine oil. Mr Blundy and Ag had got up very early. The morning before, there had been some last-minute heart-fluttering, not to say panic, because Ag's Aunt Ethel had been a long time answering Ag's letter, but come the answer did, at last, just after breakfast. All was well. The old lady in the Yorkshire Dales would be right glad of a visit and why hadn't they suggested it before now. She revealed the news about her stomach and said Ag and her husband would be a very great help and she hoped they would stay until she was able to do for herself as she had always been accustomed to do. In the meantime the district nurse was doing wonders and would post the letter for her. A visit from the Blundys, she wrote, would give her a lift.

"Blow her up like a balloon," Mr Blundy said, giving a coarse chuckle, still thinking of the gas-ter-rectumy. "Give her a real lift would that."

"Shut up, do."

On Sunday they locked up the flat for what might be a longish absence. Mrs Whale would provide the reason if anyone should enquire: doing their duty by Auntie. They drove away from Bass Street and reached Farningham at a little after 7 a.m. Mr Blundy parked the Granada. There were several other cars parked even this early.

Ag had a moan about that. "Look suspicious, we will."

"There won't be anybody around when we come out in the ambulance, Ag."

"For God's sake, They're not all going to Brands."

"It'll be okay, Ag. No need to fret. Loop knows what he's doing."

"That Bernie Harris! Not all that confident yourself, you know you're not."

"Shut up and have a suck at this." Mr Blundy produced a flask.

Ag sniffed. "Whisky?"

"Yes."

"Not usually so thoughtful, what's come over you?" Ag lifted the flask to her mouth. "Cheers, then."

"Down the hatch," Mr Blundy said, and giggled, having made a light-hearted joke to show that his nerves were okay. Just then a shadow, Old Bill-shaped, fell across the car. Just the Bill on a motorbike, all gloves and crash helmet, just having a look, that was all, but Mr Blundy didn't much like it. He gave a little shiver: omens were omens. He snatched the flask from Ag and hid it. No sense in being breathalysed, but the Bill hadn't noticed. How Mr Blundy loathed the Bill. He wouldn't piss on them if they were on fire. Traffic police in particular always looked sort of *angry* and superior and out to get you, no excuses accepted. Mr Blundy had an idea this piece of fuzz might have spotted the whisky flask after all and was being cagey, making a note of it for his breathalyser later. If that was all, well, okay, he wouldn't be taking any more sucks nor would Ag. Even so, Mr Blundy didn't feel able to relax until the Bill had scooted off. And after that, after a long trudge had taken them into Brands, there was the Bill everywhere. Foot Bill, motorbike Bill, patrol-car Bill, Bill looking after a shack where mislaid kids were taken.

Of course there was always Bill at race meetings, Mr Blundy was well aware of that, couldn't not be.

All the same, on this particular day of high endeavour and much danger, the Bill was making Mr Blundy go all funny inside. But he mustn't even think about inside.

FIVE

You could hardly move for uniforms. As if the Bill wasn't enough there were a couple of regiments of Securicor as well, roaming about inside Brands and watching the entrances and all. Making sure everyone had a stand or enclosure ticket dangling from their anoraks or T-shirts.

Mr Blundy sweated like a geyser. Place was *stiff* with the law, even chief inspectors were two a penny, just like on the real big days, now past, when the British Grand Prix had been held at Brands; and for a dead cert there would be any number of jacks, the plainclothes lot, mingling with the crowds, dressed in fashionable hair-dos of varying colours, fake racing overalls with reflective red stripes down arms and legs, or T-shirts covered with advertising gimmickry – Yardley's Toiletries for Men, say: they sold some nice lines in T-shirts at Brands, very jack-obscuring. Mr Blundy felt a cold trickle run down his spine – cold sweat, too reminiscent, or prophetic, of November in the Moor. But he managed, as he and Ag pushed through the throngs of fans and birds with paper handouts and slow-moving official cars tooting, and Bill, to induce a more hopeful feeling: if there was anything at all to be learned from the past history of crime, it was that blatant daring, such as was manifested by the Loop, did tend to produce its own reward, that the bigger the bluff the better it paid off, that the more Bill there was around the greater the likelihood of striking the target while they all got in each other's way and on each other's walkie-talkies. And on each other's tits.

51

At the paddock, no Loop.

"Now what?" Ag asked. "Your fault – being late."

"I'm not late."

Ag studied her wristwatch ostentatiously.

"Oh, leave it, Ag, do. He'll show, don't you fret."

But he didn't. Time passed. Mr Blundy's optimism took a knock. The matey, disembodied voice of the tannoy went into its day-long spiel, welcoming the crowds and running through the programme. The erstwhile stars of the racing-circuit heaven paraded in all their glory – Emerson Fittipaldi rubbing shoulders with the fans; Jackie Stewart signing autographs; Mario Andretti, Stirling Moss, Jackie Ickx *et al* beaming at their admirers who swarmed around greatness . . .

Mr Blundy gnawed at his fingernails. He'd touched Emerson Fittipaldi's overalls for luck but it didn't seem to be working. "Oh God," he said. "Something's gone wrong after all, that's for sure, Ag."

"Told you it would. But don't panic. I didn't want to come, not into this, but now we're here there's no point in panicking. Anyway, Bernie Harris, he's your friend, not mine. If he goes and lets us down, it's your fault for trusting him, which I don't, as you very well know. We'll give him another half an hour."

Mr Blundy gave her a look. "Oh, yes. Then what?"

"Then we scarper."

"Bernie'll never forgive that. Never."

"Can't help what he won't forgive. It's his – "

"Don't forget the duffers-up, Ag. They'll do us both."

"Look," she said witheringly, "if you're right and some-thing *has* gone wrong, he'll *expect* us to scarper, won't he? Not hang about to look suspicious and p'raps get him involved with the law. If he can't get hold of the kid, say, just supposing like, then it's all off till another time. Is that common sense or isn't it, eh?"

Mr Blundy blew out his cheeks. "Well, maybe. I dunno, I don't really. The Loop, he never said anything about scarpering, Ag, if he didn't show up."

"He's not as bright as he thinks he is, that one." Ag stood like a tank, glaring at a tide of stickers surging past – stickers on lunch baskets, haversacks and airline shoulder-bags, and

Bermuda shorts even, stickers colourfully advertising Team McLaren, the Constructors' Championship, Ford-Cosworth, Brabham-Yamaha and Walls Ice Cream. There was even the odd Yardley Team BRM, a hangover from former years borne proudly like old hotel or airline labels on a much-travelled man's suitcase. "Over-confidence, that's Bernie Harris's trouble. In the absence of instructions like, we got to think for ourselves."

"But what can have happened, Ag?"

She gave a short laugh, then rounded on a fan who had knocked her stomach with his elbow. "D'you mind? Talk about clumsy."

"Sorry, love." Racing fans were always polite and well behaved, not like the football hooligans.

She turned back to Mr Blundy. "Don't ask me what's gone wrong. Kid could have come up against one of them teachers. One that hadn't taken any backhanders. I don't s'pose they're all bent. Or the head teacher, he could have put his foot down, like, arrested the kid."

"They don't arrest school kids," Mr Blundy muttered. "They have another word for it. Gate them, I reckon."

Ag made a sound of impatience. "No need to go on about it, you know what I mean, what difference does a word make?"

On and on they waited. Still no Loop at eleven-forty, at which time a sound like the bombing of London in the blitz swept Brands: the first of the Formula 3000 cars were coming out for the warm-up lap. A few more minutes and more tangible evidence of the first race reached Mr Blundy: the stench of the exhaust fumes, the characteristic stench of Brands and Silverstone, Watkins Glen and Magny-Cours, Hockenheim and Monza, to the enthusiast as nectar-like as hay and horse manure to the *habitués* of Newmarket and Epsom. Today this smell bore down unheeded, swept and curled around a Mr Blundy who was on the verge of doing his nut from disappointment and fear. Having screwed himself up, having screwed Ag up as well, this was too bad. Any moment the Bill might pounce, might ask them to step along, and turn nasty if they said no. Mr Blundy's imagination blossomed: the nick, the charge room, the cells, the beak, over the bloody wall again and then maybe, if it had been *them* who'd somehow made the cock-up, the Loop waiting with his mates when they came out, all eager for the duffing up.

Mr Blundy's bowels moved horribly each time he saw a uniform.

"Where you been, then?" Mr Blundy was shaking in every limb. "Oh God, I've been that worried!"

The Loop, jaunty as ever, bung-full of confidence, put a hand on Mr Blundy's shoulder. It was now twelve-fifteen and the Formula 3000s were hard at it beyond the stands. "Little bugger. Picked him up, I did, coming out of the paddock – "

"We never saw you," Ag said angrily.

"It was early on, before you got here, Mrs B. Well, like I said, I got on to him . . . then I went and lost him. Talk about a needle in a flippin' haystack, pardon me, Mrs B. Not to worry, though, I found him again all right, a few minutes ago just. Where, you ask? In a caff, stuffing his guts. Greedy little so-and-so, but I dessay they're all the same, kids."

Mr Blundy was mopping at his face still. "Where's he now, eh?"

"There." The Loop pointed down towards the well-trodden path leading past Paddock Hill Bend. "Come on, keep close now. He's going up to Druids, shouldn't wonder."

"Which is he?"

"Bright red T-shirt with inscription 'Ayrton Senna is Magic'. Can't miss him. Washed-out jeans, but that's normal. Skinny frame, two piss-pots high, and again I ask your pardon, Mrs B." The Loop paused. "Got him, have you, Ern?"

"Yes," Mr Blundy said. "Can't exactly read the Ayrton Senna bit, not from here, like, but I think I got him, yes." He had. A boy smaller than his thirteen years looked back at that moment and Mr Blundy saw a sharp, peaky face, a cheeky look, and rather longer hair than Mr Blundy would have associated with a posh fee-paying school, but perhaps he was a bit old-fashioned. "Now what?"

"Follow. Keep with me till I say."

Mr Blundy and Ag obeyed orders. Now the moment of action had come, Mr Blundy felt a good deal easier, more professional, just like any other professional engaged in the practice of his career. It wasn't all that easy to keep track of the kid, he seemed to have a fair turn of speed, which Ag certainly had not, and at Brands everyone tended to look alike, apart from actual size and of course apart from "Ayrton Senna is Magic". Trouble was, the smaller you were, like that unsuspecting kid, the more you disappeared from view. The Loop, however, was keeping up nicely and Mr Blundy simply used him as his lodestar or leading mark. So far luck was with them: the kid was making up past Druids right enough, heading for all those nice woody parts where the deed was to be done, skipping along agilely with his phiz turned towards the exciting antics of the Formula 3000s zooming at intervals along the track and splitting all eardrums present with their intermittent racket.

The kid went on, pausing long enough to watch a close-packed bunch of cars zip past, on with the Loop behind him, down the bank behind Druids and then across the footbridge over Pilgrim's Drop.

The Loop, glancing back, gave a thumbs-up.

"What's that for?" Ag demanded.

"Means the kid's heading nice. Bit of luck, is that. Action soon now."

"Hope that Bernie Harris knows what he's doing."

"He knows all right."

They plunged on. Over the bridge, the kid turned down in the direction of Clearways, then cut left along a footpath through thick woods towards Stirling's. Once again the Loop looked back and this time halted.

Mr Blundy and Ag caught up.

"Well?" Mr Blundy puffed. He looked at Ag: she was in a bath of sweat, dress stuck to her bottom and halfway up the crack.

"This is it," the Loop said. "In the woods, he is, sooner than I thought he might. In you go, the two of you. Quick now, I don't want to see your arse for dust, Ern, and again I ask your pardon, Mrs B."

"If Bernie Harris says that again," Ag said in a fierce whisper between her teeth, "it'll be him that gets duffed up."

They overtook the boy in the shady security of the woods with no one around.

" 'Scuse me, lad . . ."

The boy turned and looked Mr Blundy up and down –
cheeky look it was and all. "Yes, what is it?"

"You lost, eh, son?"

" 'Course not."

"Well, we are." Mr Blundy, red in the face from his exer-
tions, puffed and spluttered. "This is the way to Clearways,
isn't it?"

"No, it isn't. You've taken the wrong path." The boy
pointed. "You'll have to go back the way you've come, then
turn left. Keep ahead after that and you'll come to Clearways
. . . more or less."

"Thanks, son."

"That's quite all right."

Mr Blundy looked around, somewhat idly. No sign of the
Loop, and the boy had to be retained where he was. Mr
Blundy delved in his pocket and brought out a slab of
chocolate. "Like a piece, would you?"

"That's awf'lly decent of you." The boy examined the
offering: it had suffered from the heat of Mr Blundy's body
and was all squashy and there were teeth marks where Ag had
taken a bite. "But I won't. Thanks all the same."

Just as the Loop thankfully came in sight, Mr Blundy
recognised the Kensington Gardens accent all over again.
That accent had never come from scrap iron, not by a long
chalk it hadn't. Mum and Dad were very likely dreadful
embarrassments to the kid when they showed up at that
posh school, what with dropped aitches and a lot of blimeys,
notwithstanding the Rolls, the chauffeur and the mink . . .
withdrawing the disdained chocolate from the emergent
upper classes, Mr Blundy turned to face the oncoming Loop
in his pit marshal's gear.

"Hey!" the Loop yelled as per plan. "You hear anything,
did you?"

They all shook their heads. "No," Mr Blundy said.

"You, son?"

"Only the cars." The boy was looking gratified at being
spoken to by a track official. "What sort of thing d'you
mean?"

"Sounded like a crash." The Loop, who had now reached

the group, looked all around as if baffled. "Over by Stirling's, I'd say. Quick – short cut this way." Energetically the Loop plunged into the trees and bushes. The boy's eyes gleamed and he did precisely as expected: he raced after the official-looking Loop. Mr Blundy and Ag followed. Mr Blundy, who had gone into all this with the Loop earlier when using his knowledge of Brands in his advisory capacity, knew what to do next, though his heart was in his mouth at the prospect of actually doing it. Away ahead, the Loop vanished suddenly; that was in itself the signal. The Loop would now be beating it direct for the straight between Stirling's Bend and Clearways, hot-footing it for his ready-rigged ambulance.

Mr Blundy increased speed.

Ahead, the boy plunged on through the bushes, eager to see what was to be seen, big thrill. Too bloodthirsty, Mr Blundy thought as he puffed and panted along, not right for a fan. Mr Blundy closed the gap. He was short of wind but as compared with the boy he had long legs. Coming up behind, he threw himself upon Harold Barnwell, who went down on his face – thump. Mr Blundy inhibited all cries by thrusting him deep into the tangled undergrowth. Up behind thundered Ag with the hypodermic outfit. And up into Mr Blundy's sweat-streaked face came an elbow, very effectively used in a hard backwards thrust.

"Ouch. Little bugger." Mr Blundy clasped a hand to his face and Harold Barnwell swivelled and sat up.

"What's the idea?" he asked, white faced. "You – "

"Tripped like. Now – "

"Bollocks you tripped."

Mr Blundy clicked his tongue. So that was how they talked at posh schools. "Now take it easy, son. We don't mean no harm. We – "

"What *do* you mean, then?"

Mr Blundy's mouth opened and shut again. Cor, it was all going to go wrong now and they'd be inside in a brace of shakes. He stood over the boy, wishing he could summon the will to bash him one. It was what he ought to do, of course, what any kidnapper would do, it com-ing naturally to such, but it didn't come naturally to Mr Blundy, in fact it didn't come at all. The little kid looked too defenceless. Mr Blundy dithered a bit then the big idea came. Came as though from heaven. Hoping Ag would have the savvy to back him he said, "It's your dad, son."

"What about him?"

"He don't like you going to motor races." This was safe: the Loop had spoken of the old man taking a hard line on visits to Brands. "You know that, don't you?"

"Yes, as a matter of fact I do. My father says it's a waste of time. I ought to spend my free time studying. My father wants me to be a barrister, you see, and that means good exam results, GCSE . . . which I say is for later on. But I don't understand where you two come in. Perhaps you'd better explain."

Talk about composure. There was that kid, who'd been brought down in an apology for a rugby tackle, sitting up, apparently unafraid, and lecturing his attacker. Well, he had guts. Mr Blundy sucked in air and said, "Well, first like, I didn't mean to knock you arse over – knock you down, son. Like I said – I tripped up."

No actual answer; just a sardonic stare.

Mr Blundy proceeded. "Your dad, he hired me to take you back to that school of yours."

"Are you from the police?"

"Not the police, no. Sort of private dick, like. See?"

"Or private thug. Well, in a way it makes sense. My father won't *forbid* me to go to Brands. He knows, and this I give him credit for, that my generation won't take that sort of approach. I'd come just the same, you see. I s'pose he sees this as more effective, does he?"

"I reckon he does, son, yes."

"Well, it's stupid."

"Why's that, eh?"

"He won't be able to try it on again, will he?" Eyes stared widely, all innocence.

"You mean it's a kind of one-shot?"

"Yes, obviously that's what I mean." There was impatience in the kid's tone now, suggesting he thought this bumbling private dick was a right nit. "One doesn't fall for it twice, does one? Next time I'll save up for a stand seat and stay in company . . . and set the fans on any old fool who tries to get his hooks in me, won't I?"

"Reckon so," Mr Blundy agreed half-heartedly.

"Which, of course, is what I shall do today, the moment anyone comes along – you'll not be able to keep me hidden indefinitely, will you? There's plenty of people outside these woods, you know. Don't you think you'd better clear off while you can?"

Mr Blundy felt the horrible hand of the law reaching for his shoulder. Bloomin' little classroom lawyer. Make a fine barrister, he would . . . cold-blooded, unemotional, concise – prosecution rather than defence. Mr Blundy could already see himself in the dock, being prosecuted by the little sod. By his side, Ag stirred. "Wasting time, is this," she snapped. "Get him on his face, Ern. *Go on.*"

"I can't," Mr Blundy mumbled.

"He'll yell else."

Taking the tip, he almost did. His mouth opened but Ag reacted like greased lightning. Shoving the hypodermic pack at Mr Blundy, she lunged, lost her balance and flopped down, smack on Harold, like a whale. The yell was stillborn. Harold was, in fact, badly winded; but not too winded to lash out with his feet, one of which took the hypodermic pack hard as Mr Blundy bent to examine him. The pack flew out of control and into some bushes. Giving a low moan of despair, Mr Blundy retrieved it and ferreted inside.

"All right?" Ag asked.

"No. One of the bloody phials has bust."

"Only need one for now. *Hurry up, Ern.*"

"All right, all right. Let me hold the kid, you take this lot." Mr Blundy thrust the syringe and the remaining phial into Ag's hands, feeling sick in the gut and also feeling somewhat personal about the probing needle of the injector apparatus. As Ag levered herself to a kneeling position, Mr Blundy took the boy over, holding him down by almost lying on him like Ag had. "Kick out again, sonny," he said, "and you'll get hurt. Not that I want to. Do as you're told and you'll be okay. That's a promise. Now – take your trousers down."

The boy's cheeks went a deep red. "You filthy beast," he said.

"Not *that*," Mr Blundy snapped. "What do they teach you little perishers in them posh schools?" In despair again he looked round at Ag.

Give her her due, she was quick and handy.

Already she had the hypodermic filled and, with all the expertise of a Registered General Nurse, was holding it up and squinting at it and drooling out some of the liquid until she was sure there was no air to give the kid an embolism or whatever. While she waited with the needle poised, Mr Blundy managed, with difficulty, to drag the boy's pants down and turn him on to his face so that the bared reception area was uppermost. This was the worst moment of all. It needed only some Bill with his eyes on stalks to come pushing into the undergrowth, and Mr Blundy had had it on the nastiest charge imaginable, one he would hate to go over the wall for. But now, thank God, Ag was moving into action.

"Keep him still, can't you?"

"Doing me best, aren't I." Mr Blundy was badly puffed. "Have to give me a hand, you will. One hand for the needle like. Other for the legs."

Ag muttered something beneath her breath and came down like a hefty cushion on the kid's legs. She felt around for a good entry point as practised on Mr Blundy, and from Harold there came another protest.

"Leave my bum alone, you bitch."

"I wouldn't mind betting," Ag said, "your dad pays around ten thousand nicker a year to have you taught them sordid words." Having found her spot, she shoved the needle in hard and pressed the plunger. There was a jerk and a frightened squeak, another jerk and squeak more subdued than the last one, and then silence and a notable lack of movement. Mr Blundy looked at Ag in horror.

"You put it in right?"

" 'Course. In right, and right in."

"I bloody hope so and all." Mr Blundy was shaking like a leaf. "He's gone all limp, Ag – all limp like he's *dead*!"

"Let go of him, let me have a look."

Mr Blundy got up and Ag bent. "See what you mean," she said. She rolled Harold over and pulled his pants up decently while Mr Blundy awaited her verdict. When it came, it was reassuring. "He's breathing, so don't panic. He's alive. Nasty colour, though." She lifted one of the eyelids. "All rolled round like, just the whites showing."

"Oh, God. What does that mean, Ag?"

"Means he's unconscious."

"I could have told *you* that," Mr Blundy said viciously. His own face was white with sheer fright. He gave a groan and looked all round the thickly growing trees as if hoping to find medical comforts, operating tables, consultants and sympathetic nurses emerging antiseptically from behind the exhaust-fume-weary bushes draped with wind-blown plastic beer cups, crisp packets and ice-cream wrappers. His heart was thumping so hard he believed he too needed a quack. If that poor kid should go and die . . . it just didn't bear thinking about. He and Ag would be done for murder. If it hadn't been for that needle, it could have been manslaughter, kid died of fright thinking mistakenly that he and Ag had been up to no good. But of course if it hadn't been for the needle the kid would have been okay anyhow. Oh dear, oh dear.

"The Loop, he said the kid'd just get sleepy, no more than that – that's the point, see? I don't like this, Ag – "

"He's not as bad as you think he is, Ern. That Bernie, he's too big for his boots, I don't deny, but he must have known what he was asking you to do. Wouldn't want to kill the boy, would he? Stop wetting yourself. Bernie'll be here any minute."

The Loop was not long in coming. He looked down at Harold, prodded at him, sucked his teeth a little and pronounced.

"He'll be okay, nothing to worry about. But no time to waste now." From now on till they reached the Granada in Farningham, the Loop said, he was in charge.

Mr Blundy knew he would never forget the move out from the woods with Harold's inert body being carried between himself and Ag, with the Loop leading the way to the ambulance drawn up ready on the path beyond the trees. All the comments from the gawping fans.

"Poor little kid, overcome by the heat, I s'pose."

"Looks dead to me."

61

"Don't like the look of the bloke carrying him. Could be a nutter."

"Wonder if the police have been told."

No one, however, interfered. The pit marshal's gear and the St John's uniforms on the ambulancemen were the absolute guarantees of propriety and officialdom. With Harold aboard, the ambulance was driven slowly past Clearways, through the throngs of sweaty T-shirts and mouths taking in refreshment from more plastic cups amid the roar and fumes from the circuit, down behind the hoardings with Mr Blundy suffering the awful fear of a pounce from the Bill, an arrest as they reached the exit from Brands.

He need not have worried.

The ambulance was not queried, nor was the driver's statement, made to a policeman at the gate, that he had a casualty aboard, nothing too serious, and he was taking the said casualty to his parents' car parked in Farningham for convenience of getting away after the races.

Nothing could have gone better and the Loop was beaming with pride in a job well done. Reaching the Granada, the ambulance pulled in behind, backing up, and Harold Barnwell was shoved, still unconscious, on to the back seat. Then, with the Loop aboard and heading for safety, the ambulance was driven away in the general direction of Sevenoaks. Mr Blundy took the Granada on a circuitous route for the M25, the Dartford Tunnel and the M1 for the remoteness of North Yorkshire and the hospitality of Ag's Aunt Ethel. Before reaching the motorway he pulled into a lay-by nicely shielded from the road by trees. Here Harold was bound by the arms and legs with the rope brought as a precaution, one that Mr Blundy thought it advisable to make use of from the start, seeing as the kid looked the sort to be obstreperous when he came round, if he did, and then shoved through the removable seat-back into the boot. The kid would, Mr Blundy said to Ag, be comfortable enough on his bed of pillows, blankets and eiderdown, but as he resecured the seat-back in position, Mr Blundy felt like an undertaker screwing the lid down on the coffin.

SIX

Mr Blundy drove very carefully, not wishing to shake up the contents of the boot by any lurching stops. He drove with chattering teeth, eyes staring, fingers gripping the wheel like a set of vices.

"Don't forget what that Bernie Harris said, Ern."

"When?"

"Before he left in the ambulance. He said mind to ring him after we get to Auntie's."

"I won't forget." Mr Blundy knew there was a phone box down in the village, about a perishing mile from Aunt Ethel's cottage which was itself isolated in a field behind a dry-stone wall. Once they were through the Dartford Tunnel, Ag said, "Feel like a cup of something after all that, I do."

Mr Blundy wondered how she could be thinking of cups of anything, what with what was in the boot and all. But he said, "No service areas till we're on the M1, Ag. Stop then, if you want. If you think it's safe, like. S'pose he wakes up?" He added, "I don't trust the Loop's medical know-how, Ag. Could wake any time. That's if he's not dead."

Ag considered the point. "Yes, well. Leave the cuppa, then. But there's other things in service areas. Toilets. And you'd best top up with petrol. Yorkshire's Yorkshire, not so many filling stations as down south. Not off the main roads."

"All right, then." When later a service area loomed, Mr Blundy flicked and moved into the slow lane. He pulled into the service area and circled round into the car park. Ag went off to the toilet, leaving Mr Blundy on guard, in charge of what was in the boot. Mr Blundy lit a fag and dragged on it as though it were a lifeline. His hands were shaking still. He got out of the car. His eyes, drawn as if by a magnet, stared at the boot. He wanted to open it up, to take a look, give the kid some air, but he didn't dare do that. Somebody might see, even if he grubbed through from inside, via the seat-back – you never could tell, even though he had drawn up well clear of the other parked cars, over by the railway line that ran past the car park, there were people around, mums chasing kids who had got hold of a ball, that sort of thing. People were so nosey. It would be too big a risk. Besides, come to think of it, plenty of air got into the boot. So did water, when it rained. The Granada was well past its first flush of youth.

He must curb himself, control his nerves.

Wishing he was back at contract cleaning, Mr Blundy returned to his driving seat and reached for the flask of whisky – he'd only just remembered it in all the hoo-ha. He took a big suck at the neat spirit and felt a little stronger, more able to cope with what life was throwing at him.

Ag came back from the toilet.

"All right?" she asked.

"Far as I know."

"Let's get on, then."

"I'd better have a pee, first." Mr Blundy went off. When he came back, the rear offside door was open with Ag's bottom filling it. Mr Blundy was much alarmed.

"What's up? What you doing, Ag?"

"Heard a sound. Or thought I did." Ag came out backwards. "And maybe I did, at that."

"Is he all right? Is he . . . alive, Ag?"

"Yes," she said with a degree of venom.

"You sure?"

"Quite sure. Done a pee."

"In the boot?"

"For God's sake, where else?"

"It'll *drip*," Mr Blundy said in a panic. So as to get ahead of the drip, as it were, he drove at once for the petrol pumps. Juice flowed into the tank, close to the inert form of Harold Barnwell. Mr Blundy paid cash and drove on, past a sort of shack with a sign reading "Police". Outside was a patrol car with the Bill staring him in the face from the window. Staring accusingly, Mr Blundy felt. The Bill always did, but Mr Blundy went deathly cold. The eyes seemed to be following him. But nothing could possibly be known yet. Mr Blundy looked down at the clock on the fascia: 3 p.m., just after, assuming the damn thing wasn't on the blink. The last race wouldn't finish till about four-thirty and after that it would take Master Barnwell, had he still been there, that was, a good long time to get back to that posh school of his. No alarm would be raised for a few hours yet, and even when the teachers began to get worried, probably the first thing they'd do would be to contact the kid's dad, not the Bill. All that would take time. Indeed, if the teachers had taken backhanders, they might even delay till next morning. In any case the Bill wouldn't begin to search for the boy till quite late that night, by which time Mr Blundy intended to be deep in the Yorkshire Dales surrounded by cows and horned sheep, desolate muddy roads and a good deal of open space.

Mr Blundy pulled away from the Bill, out of the service area, into the acceleration lane, flicking right. "No more stops," he said between his teeth.

"If you say so."

"Got to get to Auntie soonest possible, Ag. Though I do think we ought to take a look before long."

"At the kid, eh?"

"Yes."

"Why? What's the point in that? Nothing we can do, is there?"

"No . . ."

She gave him a sharp, sideways look. "Well, *is* there?"

Mr Blundy sighed. "No . . . no, I s'pose not."

It was soon after this that Mr Blundy's vision came to him: God, hopping about with angels around the Armco barrier. Quite uncanny, it was. But very real and very frightening, what with one thing and another. Accusing, like the Bill.

It was extraordinary. It was horribly unnerving, the more so the farther God moved north, keeping in close company. Mr Blundy's mind somersaulted, was no doubt playing him tricks. He had the thought that God had maybe come to

65

collect Harold Barnwell as the spirit emerged from the boot. The cold fingers of death seemed to settle upon Mr Blundy and for safety's sake he flicked left and shifted into the slow lane, trickling his speed down to thirty.

He wiped his face with his sleeve.

"What's up? Why slow down?"

"Christ. Jesus Christ."

"*Don't blaspheme.* You know I don't like it."

"I wasn't, Ag." It had been a simple statement of fact. He was going slower simply because of Christ, who might pounce at any moment. Mr Blundy could already be dead himself, so could Ag, there could have been an accident which sudden transference to the next world had already wiped from his awareness. He'd heard, somewhere or other, *Tit-bits* it might have been, when he'd been younger, they used to run articles on such things, written by a vicar, sort of agony vicar, he'd heard that death came like that, catching you unawares. It was entirely possible they were no longer on the motorway at all, they could be driving even now into God's kingdom, complete with boot cargo, heading up for the last reckoning.

Fanciful?

Mr Blundy's hands lathered the wheel with sweat. Of course it was fanciful, not to say daft. The wheel was there in front of him, solid and real. Ag was real enough by his side, nagging. But God was still there, haloed and now seeming to flourish something that spelled truncheon to Mr Blundy though it was more likely a shepherd's crook . . . nipping along just above the safety barrier, obscured from time to time by Long Vehicles.

It had, of course, to be just his fancy, his tormented, guilty mind.

Maybe something he'd eaten.

"I'm going bloody *mad*," Mr Blundy said aloud without meaning to.

"Eh?"

"What?"

"Said you was going mad, you did. Don't let it get on your mind, Ern. We started this, against my advice if you recall, now we've got to finish it."

"Can't finish it, Ag. It's there. *He's* there."

66

"Yes, yes, and probably sleeping quite comfy."

"What?"

"You heard."

Mr Blundy sighed. He simply could not confide in Ag, not about what he'd seen. Or thought he'd seen. She'd only call it blasphemy. There was silence for a while. Mr Blundy drove on, worrying now about the kid having peed in the boot. There could be a trail . . . but not really. All those blankets and the eiderdown would have seen to that, handy moppers-up.

"*I'll* go mad if you don't drive faster," Ag said suddenly. "Move over, do."

"No."

She drew in breath. "What d'you mean, no?"

"Ag, I'm going to pull on to the hard shoulder. I've got to take a gander at the boot."

"Don't be daft. Attract attention, that will."

"It's something I got to do. I just got to." Sweat poured down his face and he began to plead. "I *got* to, Ag. I tell you."

"Hard shoulders is for emergencies. Any police – "

"If I bloody don't I'll drive into the next car ahead."

"What's up with you, Ernest Blundy?"

Mr Blundy said no more but pulled left and stopped on the hard shoulder. Ag began a loud remonstration but he wasn't listening now. He shot out of the car, whizzed round and got in the back. Looking through the window as he reached for the rear seat-back, he had his vision again and at the same time became aware of a sort of low howl, very menacing, like he imagined a pack of wolves would sound as they closed in for the kill. He very nearly screamed: it could be the sound of death, that awful howl, coming at him out of the mists swirling over the river, Charon or Charybdis or whatever it was, Rubicon maybe . . . then he remembered.

Tyre squeal.

Them road-building buggers, why did they have to go and inflict this on him?

Trembling but relieved Mr Blundy jiggled with the seat-back. Just at that moment he became aware of panic from

Ag, who had turned round and was staring through the rear screen.

"Police," she said in a shaky voice. "Coming up behind – *get the bonnet open for God's sake.*"

Mr Blundy came out like lightning. He dashed round to the front and flung up the bonnet lid. The patrol car, flicking left, swerved on to the hard shoulder and backed up towards the Granada. The Bill got out and walked back, Bill with a peaked cap of course, the headgear that always made them more menacing and less polite than helmeted Bill. This one was heavy, slow, square-faced and with his cap-peak pulled well down over his eyes.

"What's the trouble, sir?"

Mr Blundy bet the 'sir' wouldn't last long. "Radiator, officer. Getting too hot."

"Ah. Boiling, is it, sir?"

"Reckon."

The Bill gave a nasty, cold smile, looking superior. "Coming round for the second time, are you, sir?"

"What?"

"All the way down from the north, and straight back up again? Now look, sir," the Bill said in a forbearing, patient sort of voice. "You've only just scratched the surface of the motorway so far. Cars don't boil that quick, now do they, sir? Not even bangers of this vintage." The Bill clearly didn't like the look of the old car.

"London traffic . . ." Mr Blundy said feebly.

"On a Sunday?" The eyebrows vanished up the cap-peak. "No, sir, it won't wash. It simply won't wash. I have arrived at this conclusion, sir, I do confess, not on account of whether or not you've driven near or far, sir, but on account of, if I may make an observation, you are manifestly *not* boiling. And if I may make another observation, sir, I smell alcohol."

"Oh, God."

"Yes, sir. Just wait here a moment, please."

The Bill marched back to its car. Mr Blundy's stomach turned to churning liquid. The cargo in the boot seemed almost visible, as though the boot lid were made of glass. If that nosey, sarcastic bugger poked about . . . or if Harold Barnwell began to come round . . . In sheer terror Mr Blundy watched the Bill coming back, with his mate this time, more Bill carrying the breathalyser outfit.

The gear was set up. "Now, sir. If you wouldn't mind just blowing in here, please."

Wilting more than ever, Mr Blundy blew. The Bill examined the result keenly, then looked disappointed. It hadn't been a *very* large suck at the flask, after all . . . Mr Blundy almost fainted with relief when the Bill said, "Well, sir, that seems to be all right. No excess alcohol in the blood. But I'd like you to remember it's risky to take *any* drink, however small, when driving. Now. The hard shoulder is strictly for emergency use. I'd like to know the nature of the emergency, sir. The emergency that is or was."

Mr Blundy gazed about himself, then saw Ag's distraught face glaring through the windscreen towards the group: it gave him the idea. He said, "It's the wife, officer. She wanted to go to the toilet . . . I didn't like to say . . ."

"Ah. Now, the service areas provide facilities for that purpose, sir. And out here?" The Bill waved an arm around, even more superior and cold. There was, all too plainly, no cover. "Out here, sir, that could lead to a charge of indecent and insulting behaviour. As it is, I could charge you with using the hard shoulder improperly, you do realise that, don't you, sir?"

Mr Blundy gave a humble, supplicating nod. "Yes. I'm sorry."

"That's good. Driving licence, please, sir?"

Mr Blundy produced it from his wallet. It was scanned.

"Thank you, sir. Certificate of motor insurance, please."

This also was produced from the wallet and scanned.

"Thank you, sir. MOT certificate, sir, please."

Mr Blundy's heart missed a beat then he remembered he had it with him. He fetched it from the glove compartment and it was duly scanned and handed back. "All seems to be well, sir, I'm glad to say." Bloody liar. "If you'll take my advice, sir, you'll drive on to the next service area. It's not that far. I daresay the lady can wait."

"Yes. Thank you. Er . . . you're not making a charge?"

"Not on this occasion, sir, no," the Bill said, looking into the distance over Mr Blundy's head. "Don't do it again. The motorway is for driving, not going to the toilet, sir."

"It's very good of you, officer."

"Life's too short, sir, and it's not a vital offence seeing as how an act of indecency was *not* in fact committed. If you saw all we see on the motorway, sir, you'd pack it all in and die. Good-day, sir. Kindly get back on the carriageway at once."

"Yes, of course." Mr Blundy scuttled back into the driving seat and pulled out into a nice clear stretch with his heart badly a-flutter. If that Bill had seen . . . if that Bill only knew just how close he'd been to getting his sergeant's stripes . . . but he hadn't seen and Mr Blundy knew he'd been dead lucky. In his mirror he saw the patrol car pull out behind and stay behind.

Watching.

But that Bill had been very decent really. Mr Blundy went hot and cold when he wondered whether or not his registration number had been noted. Probably had, in case he stopped again farther along. But it didn't signify, surely. There was nothing whatsoever to connect him or the Granada with reports that would emanate shortly from Brands Hatch.

Beside him Ag expelled a long breath. "Didn't I just tell you, Ernest Blundy. Don't you ever go and do anything like that again, give me a heart attack, you will. Now we'll have to go into the next service area and waste more time."

"Why, Ag? We don't have to."

"Use your loaf. That cop patrol's following – and I want the toilet, don't I, according to you?" She added witheringly, "Just shows your mental capacity, does that. Why didn't you say *you* wanted to go? Bit different for me, isn't it?"

SEVEN

After Ag's purely publicity visit to the Ladies, they lost the Bill.

Although Mr Blundy hadn't had the chance to look at Master Barnwell, they had had no actual untoward incidents when, some hours later, they left the M1 and carried on north along the M18 and then the A1(M). Just after Boroughbridge they turned off for Ripon. In Ripon Mr Blundy managed to become temporarily lost in the one-way system but eventually emerged on to the A6108 for Leyburn, whence they would head west for Wensleydale where Ag's Aunt Ethel lived her remote, lonely life.

On the road up from Ripon Mr Blundy at last had his way. It was not a particularly busy road and there was a nice lay-by not far out of Ripon.

Here Mr Blundy opened the boot.

He peered in, scared stiff at what he might see, but was very greatly relieved at what in fact he did see: Master Barnwell was alive, breathing rather hard it was true, and had a much better colour. He wasn't going to die, that seemed certain enough, and Mr Blundy flew back to the driver's seat on air.

He reported to Ag. "Still unconscious, like, but I reckon he'll be round soon."

"What did I tell you?"

Mr Blundy started up and pulled back on to the Leyburn road.

"Been out a long time he has, Ag. Could have given him more of the dope than you should."

"Why worry now, eh? Kid's all right, you said." She paused. "That Bernie Harris . . . *he* could have got the dose wrong. Not that it matters now, like I said."

"No, s'pose not."

"He's a weak-looking kid, innee? P'raps that's it, why he's taking so long to come round."

Mr Blundy nodded, feeling sorry for the kid. He'd be in a right flutter when he did come round, but he would be well looked after. Mr Blundy promised himself once again that he would see to that. Feed him up, too, on Aunt Ethel's good country fare, good Yorkshire fare. That school couldn't have done a proper job, skimped on the nosh probably, lining the head teacher's pockets. In Yorkshire they knew how to eat, none of that tinned muck. Happier now, Mr Blundy let his mind roam on food. Roast beef and Yorkshire pudding, lovely fresh greens, thick ham, plenty of milk and cheese and that. As for the food that passed for top-class nosh in the south – Greek, Eye-tie, Indian, Spanish, Frog – they could stuff it and welcome. When Mr Blundy got his cut from the Loop he might settle up here and eat good solid farm nosh, free-range eggs and all, in good, fresh Yorkshire air. If Aunt Ethel had lived down south, why, she'd have had more than gas in her rectumy . . . Mr Blundy laughed at his own unuttered little joke.

"What's funny?"

"Nothing, Ag. Just thoughts."

Ag grunted irritably but said nothing further. On the way to Leyburn they went past a number of fine-looking houses, and Mr Blundy pondered on that aspect. Really lovely houses, well built, sturdy in their Yorkshire stone, very beautiful, standing in their own large grounds, very different from Bass Street, Paddington. Butlers – they'd be sure to have butlers, and chauffeurs and maids and things. They'd have whole villages, too. Squire Blundy, good-humouredly patronising the villagers at Christmas, him as Santa Claus giving the kids presents from the Christmas tree in the big, baronial hall, with the skivvies waiting in short skirts. Mr Blundy knew that squires, after eating their Christmas fare

72

of roast beef and oxes frizzling away on spits, and plum duff with cream and brandy . . . after all that lot, they rogered the female staff, who didn't dare complain. Already Mr Blundy could feel the huge log fire warming his bottom as he stood before it, big cigar in hand, wearing a dinner suit. No doubt these big country mansions were expensive enough, but then so was Harold Barnwell, and they really did look like getting away with it now. Yorkshire was such a vast county for the Bill to comb, and chances were that the Bill wouldn't even think of looking in Yorkshire at all. Mr Blundy had no past experience of kidnapping to fall back on, but he did have a vague idea that the victims were usually spirited out of the country – how, he wouldn't know, but there it was. France, Spain, Belgium . . . anywhere, really. Far East, Australia, USA. Ports and airports watched but they still made it out. It became an Interpol job, of course, but plenty of jacks from the Yard would be living it up on their expense accounts, lucky buggers. Probably they looked forward to a really good overseas kidnap.

They passed the sign for Jervaulx Abbey. They didn't see the abbey itself but Mr Blundy knew it was a ruin and he'd visited ruins before – Fountains Abbey, also in Yorkshire, when he'd been just a lad himself, on holiday with his mum and dad, a week in a Dormobile. The place had much impressed the young Blundy with its size and antiquity, like St Paul's Cathedral only more so, and with its peace and beauty and its former total obedience to the man in charge, who his dad had said would have been like a head teacher plus extra. That day, Mr Blundy remembered now, he'd been Abbot Blundy, ruling the monks and lay brothers and whatnot with a rod of iron, really chasing them hard when they slacked off at the spud-peeling or the sluicing-down of the latrines or buggered up the making of liqueurs and that.

Mr Blundy smiled a little, inwardly. Abbot Blundy wouldn't suit him now, he was too much a man of the world, and having been inside so often he'd be ruled out in any case, probably. But it was a nice thought. When he settled down in that big house he was soon going to buy, he'd do his best to be sort of saintly short of being actually sort of *holy* . . . he would be nice to people and he would help the needy. He could even perhaps become a county figure, noted for his open-handed generosity, a friendly squire, much loved by all. And after that?

Might even become a beak. That would be a real laugh: Squire Blundy, JP! As a JP he'd be on friendly terms with such blokes as the chief constable. A little inside knowledge might be only too welcome, in case total retirement began to pall after a bit.

Then, all of a sudden, his heart hit bottom with a thump. He'd remembered something.

"Ag . . ."

"What?"

"That Mrs Whale."

"What about her, eh?"

"Knows about Aunt Ethel."

"Couldn't help but know, seeing as she took the phone call."

"Yes, I know. But she knows that's where we're going. If the Bill goes poking – "

"They won't, so keep your hair on, Ernest Blundy. The Bill don't know we had anything to do with any kidnap. They won't poke around Bass Street, got better things to do, they have."

"You sure, Ag?"

" 'Course I'm sure."

Mr Blundy's fear subsided. Anonymity was all. No leads, you were okay, you got away with it.

They drove on, turning left a little way short of Leyburn to follow a sign for Wensley.

Bang, bang.

Mr Blundy's head almost hit the roof. "What was that?"

"Boot."

Mr Blundy slowed. "Little bugger's come round," he said as there was another bang from behind.

"What you going to do?"

"See to him, that's what."

"What d'you mean, see to him?" Ag swivelled towards him. "Can't let him out, can you, and you'd better not hit him, could do some damage after that dose of whatsit – "

74

"I wasn't going to bloody hit him – "

"Take my advice and leave him be."

"But if he goes on thumping – "

Ag clicked her tongue. "It won't matter. Don't you see, it's all we *can* do?"

"Going to sound bloody funny, bang bang all the way through the villages and that."

There was another bang. It worried Mr Blundy dreadfully, did that sound, made him nervous. Ag said, "Car this age, you get bangs and thumps. And it's not all that far to Auntie's now. Go on, Ern. Forget it and speed up. Faster the better now."

He didn't like it; he dithered.

"Oh, get on do." She added, "Before he pees again."

Mr Blundy put on more speed. They banged their way through West Witton. Nobody seemed to notice; not many people around anyway, Mr Blundy was relieved to note. It was getting dark now and the Yorkshire backwoodsmen and women were not night birds, not like Paddington, it wasn't, not up here. Quite different really in what Mr Blundy had read on a sign was the Yorkshire Dales National Park. The locals probably wouldn't turn out at night even for a strip show, very likely.

Bang.

"Energetic little so-and-so," Mr Blundy said angrily. "Why can't he tire, for Christ's sake?"

"Do stop that blaspheming."

Mr Blundy said nothing. He was back to wondering about God, now far behind on the M1 as last seen. He'd not materialised since then, thank – well, yes. As the Granada left West Witton behind and moved on for Aysgarth, Mr Blundy reflected on better-authenticated manifestations. Burning bushes and such. It had been so real, so positive – that was the terrifying part. Mr Blundy hadn't much actual Bible-learning, not really, just his dad's precepts buttressed by a smattering forced into him via a curate who'd descended weekly on his primary school, which had a church foundation or something, but he had a notion that in the past God had manifested only to the righteous, to the chosen, to the workers of His will. Mr Blundy didn't rank himself among that lot. Which meant God must have made a bloomer this time. Thus the awful fear, since God just didn't make bloomers. God may have had a shift of target, so to speak, and was now showing Himself to the wicked instead, possibly with pugnacious intent.

Spoilt things, did that. Ruined the happy feeling.

"Where's the turn?" Mr Blundy asked.

"Not far. Other side of Aysgarth. Sign for Windersett."

"Know that much, don't I?"

"Why ask, then?" Ag gave a shiver. "It's lonely out here."

"Gets lonelier."

"I don't know how poor Auntie stands it, I don't. Look out, there's a sheep."

There was: before it bustled to the side of the road its eyes were like twin diamonds in the headlight beams, accusing, baleful pinpoints. Invisible but imaginable to either side rose the fells, lonely hillsides of the Pennines; now and again the headlights lit upon isolated houses, farms, cottages, and upon a rushing river – the Ure, it was – cascading over rocks large and small; and upon dry-stone walls separating the coarse, harsh ground of the fields. Outside the car the wind howled – a high wind that bent the trees and swirled dried cowpats and sheep droppings about the car. Soon there was a dash of rain, just as at last they raised the signpost for Windersett. In no time the dash became a downpour, wind-driven so that Mr Blundy's wipers almost failed to cope. It was like being in a bucket.

"That boot!" Mr Blundy said in a high voice. "Kid'll drown like as not."

As though in corroboration, the banging started again. This time Mr Blundy let it go: he was having to concentrate much too hard on his driving. Already the vicious downpour was turning the side road to Windersett – not much more than a track really – to something that felt like a mudbath. There was a horrible wheel swish. When the road began to climb Mr Blundy had the sensation of attempting to drive up a waterfall. A river of rain rushed past the car. Mr Blundy, in first gear, hoped for the best. Beside him Ag was clinging on tight, like a mountain goat, hammy hands clasped around

76

her seat. The car faltered, ground to a stop and slid back a little way, aquaplaning it felt like. Mr Blundy invoked Christ without being ticked off for it. He did some desperate work with clutch and accelerator and they crept forward again with a good deal of shudder and more banging from the boot. Mr Blundy's eyes were staring and his tongue was protruding through his teeth. He fought the old Granada's battle as though it were his own flesh and blood hauling up the climb, and he had bitten quite deep into his tongue when his headlights brought up the roof of Auntie's cottage behind the field wall on a bend of that dreadful road.

Talk about olde worlde: it was really rather nice in a way. Ag's Aunt Ethel lived totally in the past. No telly, no radio, only Calor gas to cook on. No electricity. Quaint old oil lamps – paraffin in blue Bristol glass, worth a fortune as like as not. It was a homely smell, was that paraffin lighting, even though it created an eerie atmosphere up there in Auntie's lonely bedroom in what felt like the roof of the world, a stone's throw from the great Pennine peaks. Yellow light flickered around the old lady and her high iron bedstead with brass knobs, making shadows that moved. The dim light bore witness to Aunt Ethel's methodical habits in the black carbon stain on the ceiling immediately above: the lamp always went on the wickerwork table by the right of the great bed – the great bed, according to Ag, in which not only Aunt Ethel but also her dad, her grandad and great-grandad had been born and, finally, except as yet for Aunt Ethel herself, died.

"It's nice ter see you, Aggie dear," the old lady said for the hundredth time. She hadn't yet spoken of supper.

"Nice to be here, Auntie." Ag caught Mr Blundy's eye, as if urging him to work a change of subject. Already, of course, they had enquired about Auntie's health and had had a full report on the gas-ter-rectumy and its effects upon her way of life. Also on arthritis in the hip joints, poor sight and worse hearing. Ag was already hoarse with her efforts to overcome the hearing difficulty. She glared at Mr Blundy, mouthing words.

Mr Blundy reacted. "Can we get you a bite to eat?" he shouted.

"Eh, lad?"

"Can we get you – "

"Ah'm not able to hear you, lad. Not able to hear you. Have to talk louder, you will." The pursed-up mouth, a pot-hole in a mass of crevices, wobbled into a chewing motion. "It's me ears."

"Yes. CAN WE GET YOU A BITE TO EAT?"

"Eh?"

"Stone the bloody crows."

"Eh, lad?"

Ag hissed, "Watch it. Deaf folks often hear when they aren't meant to." She leaned forward and shouted: "We was thinking about supper, Auntie."

"Eh?"

"SUPPER."

"Eh, lass?"

"Oh, leave it," Ag snapped and turned to Mr Blundy. "We're here, that's all that matters for now. We'll manage. Come on." She shouted towards the bed, "Be up again soon, Auntie."

"Eh?"

"Oh, shut up do."

"Doesn't *she* want some supper?" Mr Blundy asked.

"Don't complicate things."

"Oh, all right." They made for the door but were halted. "How long you thinking of staying?" Aunt Ethel asked.

Mr Blundy, after a glance at Ag, went back to the bedside. He bent. "Long as you want us," he shouted. "Long time no see, like – "

"Eh, lad?"

"Never mind, Auntie. We'll make up for it now. Do you proud, we will."

"Did you say a long time, lad?"

"Something like that."

"Ah. Got a nice long holiday, have you, lad?"

"Well, not exactly – "

"Eh?"

"NOT EXACTLY."

"Oh. Sorry to hear that, lad."

Mr Blundy blew out a long breath and caught Ag's eye.

78

She said, "Auntie thinks you said you'd got the sack. She wouldn't be far wrong. Anyway, leave it and come away, do."

Mr Blundy obeyed, feeling put out about the sack. They went down the narrow, steep stairs, enclosed stairs that twisted down and terminated at the door into the kitchen.

"Daft old trout," Mr Blundy muttered. "Sack, my foot."

"Oh, shut up do, I'm hungry if you aren't." Ag marched ahead into the kitchen. "She'll probably have a ham shoved away in the larder."

She paused. In the kitchen sat Master Barnwell, looking fit enough, tied with the rope to a hard upright chair, thawing and drying out in front of the Calor gas cooker, the oven of which was lit with the door standing open. There had been no fire in the living-room grate and a frozen asset was of no use to anyone. Master Barnwell had, from now on, to be pampered. Currently he was gagged in a makeshift way with a handkerchief and a wedge of Sorbo that Mr Blundy had pulled off a pad which he normally used for demisting the Granada's windscreen. And, since he always washed out the pad afterwards in detergent, Master Barnwell was frothing a little.

"What do we do with him now?" Ag asked.

"Got to eat."

"That's what I meant."

"Oh. Take the gag off, Ag?"

"Yell the place down, he will."

"So what? The old besom'll only think it's the wind." The wind was bad enough as it was: the whole cottage shook and rattled and there was a constant whine in the trees without. "No one else around to hear, is there?" Mr Blundy moved towards the bound boy. "Hear what I said, did you, son? This place is dead lonely, dead remote like, miles and miles from anywhere, and it won't do you no good to yell. Waste of breath, that's all. Just the same, like, the wife and me, we don't like noise. So don't yell, all right? Yell and you get duffed up. Behave and you'll live off the fat o' the land. Understand, do you?"

The head nodded briefly.

"We don't want to hurt you, son. I *mean* that. Too

79

valuable." Mr Blundy reached out and unfastened the knot of the handkerchief, letting it go and pulling the Sorbo out of the boy's mouth. "There. Now just remember all I said, son."

Master Barnwell took several deep breaths and then spat. "Dirty little bugger."

"Not as dirty as you, whoever you are." The lips were trembling now, but with anger and bad temper, Mr Blundy fancied, rather than fear. "You're villains, aren't you?"

"Don't be rude."

"I was speaking in a police sense. To the police, you'll be villains."

"Now look – "

"My father didn't send you. My father doesn't know anything about you, does he?"

"Hope not," Mr Blundy said.

"You've kidnapped me, haven't you?"

Mr Blundy smiled placatingly. "What if we have? Your old man's rolling in it, like a pig in mud. You'll soon be back home, you'll see. Just look on the bright side, son. You're here and you're staying till your dad pays up. Look on it as a sort of adventure, like, eh?"

Master Barnwell studied him. "You won't get away with it, you know. You can't. Kidnappers always come to a sticky end. The police'll be looking everywhere."

Mr Blundy sniggered. "Not here, they won't."

"Where are we, then?"

"Never you mind about that."

"You're not going to tell me?"

" 'Course not. We're not daft, son."

Harold Barnwell said no more, but there was a curious sort of glint in his eyes that rather worried Mr Blundy, though he couldn't quite put a finger on the reason. The kid couldn't possibly know where he was – they were safe enough on that score, surely? Mr Blundy shook his head and thought about the Loop as Ag marched around getting supper. Mr Blundy had yet to telephone the Loop to confirm their safe arrival at Auntie's and maybe get some news as to what the Bill was up to, if anything. Until Mr Blundy had made contact, the Loop would naturally not be advancing his part in the programme.

"Going to phone, Ag."

"Know where it is, don't you?"

"Yes." Mr Blundy went out into the hostile night, becoming drenched in seconds. Plunging through mud towards the village, Mr Blundy found the phone box on its corner. Unoccupied, thank God, no one would want to be out on a night like this. The Loop answered right away and very circumspectly.

"Yes?"

"Me."

"Ar."

"Got here."

"Right." Click. No news from the Smoke, it seemed. No mucking about on the part of the Bill. Already the trail would be going cold. So far, so good.

Mr Blundy went back for supper.

He thought about the Loop. Now that the Loop knew that Harold Barnwell was safely stowed away amidst mud, sheep, cows and Auntie, and that nothing had gone wrong en route, he would be all set to start putting the squeeze on the kid's dad. This important part of the work-out had not been revealed to Mr Blundy in any detail, but the Loop's part would obviously be dangerous, because Mr Barnwell might report any cash demands to the Bill, and the Bill might set a trap, into which the Loop might walk if he wasn't dead careful. The Loop had said, rather casually, that he *would* be dead careful and Mr Blundy could rely upon that. He had, he'd said, ways and means – besides which, as he had repeated once again, Barnwell Senior doted on the kid and could easily part with the cash, no problem there. And if the threats were phrased right he would, in the Loop's view, be highly unlikely in fact to say anything to the Bill about kidnap notes. The poor Bill, all unknowing of the truth, would go on combing the woods at Brands and parts adjacent and dragging ponds and whatever, harassing all known nutters in Kent and probably East Sussex. While they were thus engaged, the Loop would collect. The split would be made with Mr Blundy and Master Barnwell would be taken down the M1 again and set free somewhere in outer London with no knowledge whatsoever of where he'd spent the period of detention.

Nothing could possibly go wrong.
Cast iron, it was.

Back at Auntie's, Ag said, "Come and get it, then. I'll feed the boy." Suddenly she froze. "What's that?"

A creak on the stairs. "Auntie," Mr Blundy said, going white. "Hide the kid, quick." He leapt towards Harold, shoving a hand over his mouth just in time to stifle a yell. "Where'll we put – "

"Leave him. I'll head off Auntie." Ag was already moving for the door of the boxed-in staircase; Mr Blundy watched her vanish, heard her remonstrating voice.

"Now what d'you want to go and get up for, Auntie, gas-ter-rectumy an' all, it's daft is that – "

"Eh?"

"GO BACK TO BED."

"Me sooper, lass. Me sooper. Not that I want mooch – "

"I'LL BRING IT OOP. UP."

"Eh?"

"Oh God. Just do as you're told, Auntie, like a good old lady, we're here now and we'll do for you – "

"Eh?"

"DO FOR YOU. Will and all if this goes on, shouldn't wonder. HAVE A GOOD REST WHILE YOU CAN."

"Eh?"

There was a hissing sound from Ag but no further speech. The next sounds were of physical activity: Auntie was being returned to bed more or less forcibly. Then a door banged shut; this was followed by muted sounds from Ag, after which she came down looking red and sweaty. "That's all right," she said, breathing hard. "She'll stay put. Now where were we?"

"Supper."

"Oh yes, supper. Auntie's on liquid nourishment."

"Can't keep going on that."

"She knows her own stomach best – "

"Hasn't got one, Ag. Taken out. Gas-ter-rectumy, like you said."

"Well, I haven't the time to go into that, not now."

Ag busied herself filling the plates. Mr Blundy sat down

at the big scrubbed-wood kitchen table, obviously Auntie's pride and joy, poor old trout. Mr Blundy, wondering when she would be allowed to see it again, ate ham slices and bread and butter with a good appetite and washed it all down with hot, thick cocoa. Ag, after she had taken the old lady's liquid meal up, sat beside Harold Barnwell and thrust ham into his mouth. The kid, Mr Blundy thought, was doing himself pretty well in spite of what must be, or ought to be, any road, his fear and anxiety as to his future. After some cocoa had been poured in, his face seemed to glow with health – the air, of course, was keen and invigorating up here in the Dales and was doing him good already . . . Mr Blundy gave a rather maudlin smile. He said kindly, "Nothing to fret about, son. Just fill your boots. You'll be nicely looked after. The missus and me, we like kids, see. That's right, eh, Ag?"

"Yes." Ag shoved in more cocoa from the mug. "Anything else you'd like, is there?"

"No."

Mr Blundy sat back, smiling still, nodding a little to himself. It was a homely scene, much more homely than he'd ever known it to be in Bass Street, Paddington. The cottage kitchen, the good air, the ham and bread and butter, the warmth from the Calor gas oven . . . pity about the wind and rain but all in all it was the good life out in the country, no doubt about that, and what with the kid, and Ag looking quite motherly considering . . . it was great. They might even miss Harold when he had to be decanted back into London's roar. Depended how long before the Loop got results, of course, but the lad could even come to miss them and this nice homely scene when he went back to that posh school and all the teachers chivvying him around, do this do that, and the bell and all, maybe the cane. They were all sadists in the posh schools, never stopped caning and never mind the law on kids' rights . . .

Mr Blundy became aware of Harold's eye on him, glinting again. Talk about disconcerting: not for the first time in his life Mr Blundy reflected on the self-confidence that came from being rich. He asked pleasantly, "What's on your mind, son?"

The glint increased. "You."

83

"Me?"

"Yes, you. You're both amateurs, aren't you?"

Mr Blundy's face reddened. "Eh?"

"You both seem what I'd call unprofessional. I'm sorry if I seem rude, but that happens to be the impression you're giving me."

"Cheek!" Ag said, glowering. "Just you shut up and remember where you are."

The boy nodded off-handedly. "Yes. I say . . . that boot of yours. It's a frightfully old car, isn't it?"

"No business of yours," Ag said.

Harold disregarded her. "I expect your idea is to abandon it when and if you get the ransom money."

Mr Blundy set his lips. The homely scene was evaporating – and there was truth around. Already it had been agreed that the old Granada would become totally lost after Harold had been handed back. Just a precaution, of course, but it was nasty that the facts of kidnap should be so closely approached by the victim. Harold went on with an air of amused detachment. "About time, I'd say. That boot – awf'lly wet and draughty. Awf'lly dismal drive." He paused, surveying them with a lofty air. "Other things too."

"Eh?" Mr Blundy stared. So did Ag.

"M18," the boy said with relish. "Boroughbridge. Ripon. Wensleydale. Windersett."

"You – "

"Aunt Ethel."

"*You little – *"

"Walls, as I'm sure you know, have ears. So have boots. Specially your boot. You must have a split seam like a coal mine down the back seat. And you did talk rather loudly, didn't you?"

Mr Blundy shook. "Eavesdropping little bugger."

"Well, as I said, you know – amateurishness. It's that element that's going to get you caught. It's so awf'lly stupid."

"Look," Mr Blundy said in a high voice, having just had a suspicion, "you ever been kidnapped before, have you?"

Harold Barnwell smiled, craftily, Mr Blundy thought. "Yes, I expect you'd like to know that. But I shan't tell

84

you. If I have . . . well, the police are going to jump to certain conclusions this time, aren't they?"

Mr Blundy, watched by Ag, got to his feet and walked up and down the kitchen, kneading his fingers nervously, back and forth past the Calor gas oven and its open door, thinking and thinking and becoming more and more worried as a result. Surely the Loop would have known about any previous kidnaps, it would be his job to investigate such things. That stood to reason. No, it was eye-wash, just a case of the kid trying to get them rattled once he, Mr Blundy, had given him his opening by asking the question.

Amateurs!

Bloody cheek.

Amateurs at kidnapping maybe, but not at crime and the ways of the criminal and dodging the Bill.

Mr Blundy stopped his pacing and looked down at Harold Barnwell, smug little brat he'd turned out to be. "Now look, son. It may come as a surprise to you to know I've been inside more times than – "

"*Ernest Blundy!*"

Mr Blundy jumped a mile. Ag looked shattered at her own indiscretion. Harold Barnwell gave a shriek of laughter, a real four-ale-bar guffaw. "Ernest Blundy. That's going to be very useful to know, isn't it? I did say, didn't I, that you're a couple of amateurs."

Mr Blundy shook with fear and anger. "Made a bloomer yourself, haven't you?"

"Oh? How?"

"*Telling* us you know where you are. Daft, that – amateur-ish. Now we know you'll be able to shop us after, eh? Lead the Bill to that poor old lady in bed upstairs – "

"The poor old lady you spoke of as the old besom and the old trout?"

Mr Blundy waved a fist in front of the boy's nose. "Don't push your luck, son. Think we're going to have you talking to the Bill, which is what you'll go and do, isn't it, eh?"

"Not necessarily." Was there a touch of the scares now? "It depends whether or not you treat me properly. While I'm in your clutches."

"Ah – like that, is it? I said you'll be treated proper.

And you would have been. Different now, innit, eh? Very different – could be. Could be we collect and then do you in for safety's sake. Didn't think of that, did you? Daft little kid. Ever heard of High Force, have you?"

"Yes. Forty-foot waterfall. Near Middleton-in-Teesdale. I've been there. It's on the road to Alston, which is the highest – "

"All right, all *right*. May go there again and all," Mr Blundy said, sounding really savage. "May get chucked in and bloody *decimated* on the rocks under if you don't watch out."

"Rubbish," the boy said calmly.

"Rubbish? Daft little – "

"Because kidnappers never collect unless and until the victim is handed over, for one thing. For another, neither you nor the fat woman are murderers."

"Oh, yes?"

"I've read somewhere," Harold Barnwell said in a superior tone, "that the photographs of all murderers, and I repeat *all* murderers, and murderesses, show one feature in common: the eyes are on very slightly different levels, one set a shade higher than the other. Your eyes are not, neither of you." He shook his head, smiling. "*You* won't kill me . . . so don't try to scare me that way. It simply won't wash."

EIGHT

"Little devil."

"Fat woman," Ag said in an angry hiss. She flopped over in the bed, to fan Mr Blundy's ear with heavy breathing. "Such *cheek*, kid of that age! How long before this ends, I'd like to know."

"Have to wait for the Loop, Ag."

"Go on for ever, most likely."

"Now look, Ag." Mr Blundy sat up in the bed. "Things we have to sort out. One of us must be here all the time. Can't go out together, see? And don't let the old bag come down the stairs, not ever, not so long as we're here. Keep her in bed. Do her gut and rheumatics good, will that. Look after the poor old soul. What she don't see – "

"Yes, all right, don't go on and on. I know what I have to do. I just hope *you* do. Sure that kid's okay for the night, are you? Wet, in the outside bog."

"He'll be all right so long as he don't drop down the hole. Auntie's got her commode so I reckon he won't get disturbed. And I put the gag back on, not that anyone's likely to hear his noise."

Ag grunted and turned her body back the other way. That outside bog . . . Yorkshire men and women were tough, had to be to withstand earth closets, but the kid had been brought up posh and soft like. "Give him the blankets and pillows, did you?"

" 'Course I did." Mr Blundy added with an invisible grin,
"You getting fond of him or something?"

"Not when he calls me the fat woman."

Next day was lovely: clear blue skies with little fluffy white
clouds scudding helter-skelter over the fells, the wind fresh
rather than overpowering. Up and up rose the Pennine
peaks, green and grey and mauve, with little sparkling
streams running down the gills towards the river. It was
a real pleasure to be driving along the A684. Mr Blundy
hummed a little tune to himself: he was on top of the world,
mentally as well as physically.

Last night, at 0234 hours, this morning really, a miracle had
taken place.

There had been sex.

It was really amazing how quickly the human body reacted
to the Yorkshire air. Sex had become almost unprecedented
in Mr Blundy's life. He had made Aunt Ethel's spare double
bed shake and rattle like one of those old London trams his
dad used to tell him about. The brass knobs had jiggled
and spun like all-get-out and he'd wondered what Aunt
Ethel would have thought had she been able to hear. And
after that, the wonderful morning stealing through the little
window – lovely! Even the BBC news broadcast on Ag's
transistor hadn't been too alarming, no more than had been
naturally expected: a kid had been reported missing after the
racing at Brands and the Bill was on the look-out down south,
but there was no mention of any possible kidnap and listening,
as it were, between the lines, Mr Blundy guessed the Bill was
dead flummoxed for leads.

After the news, ham and fried eggs for breakfast and a visit
to the outside commode to see to Harold. The kid, Mr Blundy
found, was cold but fit, sitting tied to a heavy iron ringbolt set
in the closet's one stone-built wall, the others being of wood.

"Don't s'pose you've ever seen this sort of toilet," Mr
Blundy remarked as he removed the gag. "Primitive, they
are, up here, like."

"Oh, I've seen them. As a matter of fact we have them at
Haverstock."

Mr Blundy was very surprised. "You do?"

"Yes. Only we call them lavatories. Haverstock's a very old place with big grounds. In the old days, the servants used the earth lavs outside. Some of them had three seats in them."

"Cor. Not used now?"

Harold shook his head. "Only to play hide-and-seek in. We go down on a rope."

"With all that dried . . ." Mr Blundy shook his head in amazement at how the other half lived. "Reckon there's higher standards down Wapping way. Never know how the nobs live, do you, eh."

"We don't *live* down there," Master Barnwell said in a superior tone. "I can't speak for you and Wapping, of course."

"Don't be so rude. Don't be so toffee-nosed neither." Mr Blundy wagged a fist. "Don't want to be duffed up, do you?"

Harold clicked his tongue. "What a stupid expression – duffed up. Old-fashioned, too, isn't it? I imagine you're one of the illiterates we read so much about. Are you going to cook me some breakfast, or is the fat woman?"

"Don't you go on about the fat woman. I don't like it."

"Sorry. Anyway, I'm awf'lly hungry. I'd like bacon and eggs. Lightly fried. Then toast and marmalade. Coffee, of course, not tea."

"You'll be bloody lucky, I don't think, Your Lordship – "

"I expect you drink tea."

"Yes, I – "

"The working classes do."

"Cocky little bastard. You'll go hungry for all I care."

"Oh?" Harold lifted an eyebrow. "I call that very short-sighted."

So, in point of fact, did Mr Blundy. Harold had to be kept nourished. He aimed a swipe at the kid's head and went back to the cottage and told Ag the kid would like ham and eggs the same as them.

"Where's he going to eat it?" Ag asked, busy at the Calor gas stove. "Not out there, is he?"

"Don't see why not."

"If you don't, Ernest Blundy, I do. Catch things – it's not hygienic. Don't want him ill, do we?"

"All right. Have him in. But guard the stairs against Auntie coming down."

" 'Course." Ag paused, breaking another egg into the frying-pan. "Can't go on too long, can't that. Been thinking like. She's going to smell a rat soon. Auntie's never been one to take to her bed, not for long she hasn't."

Mr Blundy laughed. "Going to have to be, now."

"Nor one to take orders."

"We'll see about *that*," Mr Blundy said, steeling himself.

Ag stopped frying and turned on him, hands on hips. "What's come over you all of a sudden, getting all bossy?"

"Yorkshire."

"Well, I wonder. Maybe it's too much you-know-what."

Mr Blundy gaped. "*Too much?* Once after I don't know how many years and you call it too much – "

"Oh, don't go on about it, sound like one of them sex fiends you do. Gives you ideas of being like masterful . . . getting on top of me like that. Self-control's a blessing if you give it a chance. By the way, you'd best blindfold the kid before you bring him out in the open, right?"

"Right," Mr Blundy said, using self-control.

Alas for human frailty, every dog has his day but it doesn't necessarily last all that long. Mr Blundy's didn't last the morning. Breakfast over, he'd had something nagging at his mind, he didn't know why, it just did. A kind of premonition. Thus on that lovely bright morning, still thinking of the you-know-what during the night, he'd driven into Hawes, leaving Ag behind with the kid, to put through another phone call to the Loop. He wouldn't ring again from Windersett, not so soon after the last call, because you never knew and the Bill might be more wily than he gave them credit for.

Mr Blundy returned along the A684 from Hawes in a bitter and fearful frame of mind.

God, how unlucky could you get?

Already he felt the hand of the Bill upon his shoulder, saw the nick gates close, heard their forbidding thud. How many years for kidnap?

The wonderful morning had gone, literally. Once again, rain gushed from above the Pennine Chain, cloud sat fast on Mr Blundy, gluing itself to his windscreen. Yorkshire, suddenly and viciously turning its worst face. Mr Blundy lived in a diving bell. All misted up inside and the bloody Sorbo pad left back at Auntie's for use on the kid. He drove cautiously, peering and peeking, half expecting the Bill to show through the mountain mists. When at last he made the turn for Windersett, just seeing the sign before he hit it, he was almost gibbering to himself. Reaching Auntie's lonely cottage, he shoved the car round the back, running it into the broken-down barn that he'd used the night before.

As he approached the back door into the kitchen he heard sounds of anger.

Ag.

"Give me any more of your cheek and I'll do you, rotten little pest!"

Mr Blundy entered to see Ag's arm raised and her big face red as a turkeycock, and Master Barnwell, bound but ungagged, smiling with cautious disdain from his hard upright chair. Mr Blundy noted that the kitchen window was curtained; evidently Ag had decided Master Barnwell was not to see an identifiable dale or fell, an unnecessary precaution in Mr Blundy's view now that the little sod had already spoken of Windersett, but still.

Ag lowered her arm and said, "Oh, you're back."

"Am and all. I – "

"I can't stand much more of that little horror. I can't put up with his cheek – "

"I always thought," Harold said innocently, "that fat people were placid."

"There – see?" Ag raised a fist again. "I've had a dreadful morning, really dreadful, Ern."

"Put him back in the bog," Mr Blundy said reasonably. "With his gag on."

"It's all very well you – "

Masterfully, since having been accused of it he might as well act up, Mr Blundy moved towards the upright chair and made to replace the gag and blindfold.

"Just a moment," Harold said with that unwelcome gleam back in his eye.

"What?"

"I just thought we might have a chat about motor racing. You're a fan."

"S'pose I am. So what?"

"Who d'you support?"

"Nigel Mansell."

Harold made a rude noise. "Ayrton Senna's the greatest."

"No he's not. Nigel Mansell – "

"Nigel Mansell couldn't drive a bus. I bet you were pretending to be Nigel Mansell when you drove up here, weren't you? I mean, you can't drive either. Nigel Mansell – "

"Any more out of you," Mr Blundy snapped, "and you'll get duffed up, all right?"

"Not that silly expression again. I repeat, Ayrton Senna's the greatest – "

"Nigel Mansell, he knocks spots off – "

"Oh, leave him, do." This was Ag, large and angry, looming close. "Can't you see, he's only trying to gain time out of the bog? You'd fall for anything, you would, call yourself intelligent? *I* dunno . . ."

"All right, all right." Mr Blundy seized gag and blindfold again and reapplied them to Harold. Slacking off the rope binding the boy to the chair, he lifted him, got him on the move for the door and bundled him out towards the earth bog. "Ayrton Senna my backside," he muttered balefully as he secured Harold to his ringbolt and came out stern first. Locking the door, he returned to the kitchen, his face working with anger and anxiety, and when he got there he saw that he'd got the kid out just in time: Auntie was down again.

Ag was already pushing her towards the stairs. Auntie was saying pathetically that she didn't like staying in her bed, she didn't.

"Always been active, like, Aggie dear." Thin white hair hung wispily and patchily around the wrinkles of the face and neck. "Stay in bed and t'rheumatics catch oop with you . . . them or t'bedsores."

"Never you mind that," Ag yelled in her ear. "What you want is rest. Had a hard life you have, you know you have – "

"Ernie," the old lady said, catching sight of Mr Blundy just as she reached the stairs under propulsion. "Ernie, tell 'er to let me be. Tell 'er it's *my* 'ouse like."

92

Mr Blundy sweated. He had his own worries, hadn't he? More, much more since that phone call from Hawes. "You're best off in bed," he shouted. "BEST OFF IN BED. Ag's right. We'll look after you, just see you take it easy like." His anxieties sharpened his tone. "Go on now, up you go."

"Eh?"

"Shove her," Ag said, pushing Mr Blundy out of the way.

The old lady seemed about to burst into tears. Mr Blundy felt mean and cruel but contrived to look severe and determined. Aunt Ethel was shoved nearer the stairs which she climbed slowly with Ag behind her. Mr Blundy waited in increasing impatience; when Ag came back down she started on him but he cut her short.

"You gotta watch what you do to the kid now – "

"Oh, shut up, do. I can't stand any more being *got at*. What with the kid and you and Auntie and her stomach . . ." She looked more closely at his face. "What's up, eh?"

"Everything." Mr Blundy breathed hard. "Look, your aunt – "

"Been creating all morning, she has. Bang bang with her stick. *I've* had her, not you."

"She can create all she bloody likes, Ag, but for God's sake keep her upstairs, tell her she's sick, anything, she looks bloody sick and all. Any road, she's to stay in bed. I got enough to worry about."

Ag made a hissing noise. "Well, come on, then, tell me."

Mr Blundy shook his head and looked despairing. "It's bad, Ag. The Loop – I got another bloke when I rang. Don't know who he was – "

"Didn't you ask?"

"Wouldn't say. Said the Loop wasn't there." Mr Blundy mopped at his face. "He's a goner, Ag."

She stared. "Goner? Who?"

"The Loop. Copped it – dead. As a bloody doornail. Car, see. Head-on crash into one of them big Volvos. During the night, it was, when we were – "

"Yes, all right." Ag sat down hard. "Oh, my God. Where does that leave us, eh?"

"Up the bloody creek, of course, where d'you bloody

think? I just don't know how to cope on me own, Ag, it's all too big."

"Told you that from the start, didn't I, but oh no, you wouldn't listen, thought you – "

"Didn't ever think this would go and happen, did I?" Mr Blundy, shaking like a leaf, dropped on to a chair and put his head in his hands. "Oh, God. I've no experience. I don't know how to put that sort of squeeze on, chat up a bloody millionaire so he parts with half his bloody fortune."

"Never know till you try."

"Come off it, Ag. We've had it. I can't be in two places at once anyway. Need to be here to guard the kid, don't I? Can't leave it all to you, what with your aunt and all – "

"Shut up and don't panic," Ag snapped. "Look: that bloke you said you spoke to, on the phone. Can't he come in on this? Handle Bernie's end?"

" 'Course not. Fix that sort of thing up on the phone? Don't be daft."

"Not on the phone, no. Go and see him, down the Smoke."

Mr Blundy shook his head. "Too risky. How do I know I can trust him, or anyone else come to that? Don't you bloody *see*? We *can't* talk to anyone, not *anyone*. We don't know who the Loop had in with him on this. It'd be suicide." He said it again for emphasis. "Bloody suicide."

"We got to do something."

"But what, Ag? What do we do?"

"We act like a man to start with," Ag said energetically, "that's what. Far as I see, there's two things we can do. One, you leave the kid with me, it'll be difficult but I'll manage when I have to, and you get yourself down the Smoke, like I said already, and – "

"Find this bloke, I s'pose. I said – "

"Not the bloke, no. I know what you said. Contact this Barnwell. Kid's dad. Think up some way of making a safe exchange – you're not that daft and helpless, or are you?"

"I've no *experience*," Mr Blundy said pathetically, and added, "not in kidnap. Like all lines, you got to start small and work up big, see . . ."

"Like kidnapping tadpoles first off, I s'pose?" Ag sneered.

"Work up to cats and dogs. Then people. You make me sick, you do. All your airs and graces, yack on and on about all you're going to be, all them big houses and cars and that, so much lolly you don't know how to eat and drink it fast enough. You're all wind and piss, Ernest Blundy, that's what you are. Air balloon, now pricked. God give me strength. All you're fit for is contract cleaning and you made a hash of that too, couldn't stand the pace."

"Don't be so unfair," Mr Blundy said in a whine. "I had an awful – "

"Oh, shut up. Go on being gutless." Ag swung her bottom towards him, then turned back again. "I said, didn't I, there's two things we can do. Right?"

Mr Blundy nodded.

"Want to hear what the second thing is?"

"Go on, then."

"We give in. We hand the kid back, with thanks." Ag's big chest heaved. "I'd be glad enough to get rid of him and that's a fact. If it wasn't for the money."

"Well, you can't," Mr Blundy said. "That's the one thing we can't do whatever happens. Remember? Little bugger knows we're round Windersett way. No matter where we take him and dump him, he's going to send the Bill right in and they're going to question your Aunt Ethel along with everyone else around and then we've had it, haven't we? Can't even silence the old bag by doing her in, can we? That way we'd get done for murder as well as kidnap."

"Aunt Ethel don't know there's a kid here."

"No," Mr Blundy agreed, "she doesn't, that's true. But she knows *we're* here, and she knows where we live, and when the Bill comes round with their bloody interrogations and that, she yacks – right? Then *we* do the answering. Unless we can vanish. Not easy it isn't, to vanish. Not with the Bill hot on the scent. And there's one thing we can't ever skate round, isn't there? When the Bill shows us to Master bloody Barnwell, the little sod *recognises* us, don't he?"

"Would have been the same anyway, once we'd got the money – "

"No it wouldn't, 'cos then we'd have had the cash to vanish proper, like out of the country."

Ag was staring at him, wide eyed. Something had struck home, a number of pennies, one in particular, had dropped with a bang. "Mean to say, do you, we're stuck with that wretched kid?"

"Stuck's the word. For life by the look of it. Can't hand him back. Can't cash him in." Mr Blundy, who had lifted his head from his hands long since in order to make his points to Ag, thrust it back again and slowly shook it from side to side. "I just don't know what we're going to do. Honest I don't. Not got a lot of the readies left, we haven't. I been banking on the Loop." He looked up sharply, leaving the cover of his hands, eyes narrowed. "How's your Aunt Ethel fixed, eh?"

"Got a few bob in cash tucked away, shouldn't wonder."

"Worth bearing in mind. Borrow it maybe."

"Borrow it?" Ag loomed over him. "Ask first, mind."

"Don't be daft, she probably wouldn't part."

"Now look," Ag said aggressively, "she may be an old cow but she's my own flesh and blood. I don't reckon to – "

"Leave a bloody IOU, won't I?" Mr Blundy said, sounding aggrieved. "It's sink or swim, no time for going all sentimental and – "

"Oh, shut up, do." Ag went off on a different tack. "Look, how about the papers, eh?"

"Papers?"

"Newspapers. Had a look, have you, in Hawes?"

"Bought a *Mail* and an *Express* and a *Telegraph*. Nothing – not even the Late News. Be in tonight's, I reckon, down south. We'll get it in tomorrow's dailies. The kid and the Loop, poor sod." Mr Blundy's chest suddenly tightened into a horrible constriction and his face grew deathly white. The Loop . . . that terrible squashed end during the night . . . true, it hadn't happened while he, Mr Blundy, had been driving up the motorway, but the foreknowledge in heavenly circles that it was going to happen soon could have accounted for the flitting presence of God, a vengeful and mocking God, a God about to deny all shelter and safety to wicked Mr Blundy, as wicked as the Loop . . . which was maybe why He had been so pointedly using the safety barrier as his rostrum, or pulpit. Making a very definite point.

There would be no safety now.

Oh God.

"He's impossible," Ag said. Her initial anger and scorn had muted, after some repetition over the midday meal. Now she was more chatty, seeking sympathy. "Gets on my nerves, he does. I won't be able to take being stuck with him, I won't." She sucked in her lips. "Know what?"

"What?"

"Quotes bleedin' Shakespeare at me. While you was seeing to the car. 'I will feed fat the ancient grudge I bear you,' Merchant of somewhere, Venice, was it? 'Falstaff sweats to death and lards the lean earth as he walks along.'" She glanced up at him, across the ham. "What was this Falstaff, Ern?"

"Dunno really," he answered vaguely. "Fat bloke, I reckon . . . very fat, like."

"I thought so and all. If I'd had a kid, I'd never have sent him to one of them private schools. So rude. Why, he even brought arithmetic into it. Just to get at me."

"How's that, then, Ag?"

"Can't really remember, like . . . something about being cubed. I don't know. I do know it was meant to be rude. And something about a barrel and a fuckin. Such language for a little kid."

"Firkin," Mr Blundy said absently. "Not fuckin."

"Oh. Well, yes, he did say firkin but I thought he meant the other. What's firkin?"

"To begin with," Mr Blundy explained wearily, "it's not firkin, it's *a* firkin. It's not a bloody verb like the other. What it is . . . oh, barrels, firkins, hogsheads and that. Beer measure, I reckon."

Ag looked at him shrewdly, as if surprised, which she was. "Better educated than I thought, you are. *You* talk to the little blighter. On his own level. Take him down a peg or two. I'm sick of him, keeping on getting at me."

"He's not a bad kid, Ag. Not bad at all. Bright little face. Got guts too . . . all right, all right," he added quickly, anticipating Ag's anger. "Look. If he keeps getting at you, why don't *you* answer him back? Never known you short of something to say."

"Comes back with something better every time. I'll clout him one if he goes on."

There was a silence. Ag got up to make a pot of tea, the working-class drink. Gloomily Mr Blundy stared at her bottom, and past it through the window towards the Pennine peaks, now just visible again as remote grey shadows breaking through the mist and rain. Yorkshire's lustre had dimmed in more ways than the one. Mr Blundy could have cried. It wasn't fair, it wasn't bloody fair at all after all his efforts. No provision had been made against the Loop's death, which had been a totally unforeseen catastrophe. Mr Blundy was knocked endways up.

The tea made, Ag came and sat at the kitchen table again and poured three cups.

"Take one up to Auntie."

"All right. Keep her sweet. What about the kid?"

"Sod the kid. You said he said tea was common. Have to go without, little snob."

Mr Blundy shoved Auntie's cup on a small tray along with a bowl of sugar and twisted up the steep stairs to the old lady's bedroom. Auntie was lying there like death, white and still and silent but with her eyes wide open and apparently staring through the window opposite. Mr Blundy coughed but failed to penetrate the brick wall of deafness. He placed his body and his tea-tray in the old girl's line of sight, between bed and window, but still nothing seemed to register.

"Bloody dead and all," Mr Blundy said aloud. The tea-tray rattled in his hands. More trouble. Get the quack in, and the undertakers, and things would start coming out. It was really too bad. Mr Blundy went slowly closer to the bedside table and put the tray on it. Fearfully he reached out to Auntie's chest, which looked horribly still like the rest of her and which was concealed beneath throat-high material, coarse like calico. He laid a hand over the region of her heart.

Aunt Ethel was not dead.

At the first touch she gave a jerk of the head and body, turning short-sighted eyes towards Mr Blundy.

"Well I never did."

Mr Blundy cleared his throat.

"How *dare* you?"

"Sorry, sorry – "

"What a thing to do. Must 'ave gone crazy."

Mr Blundy, his face flaming, stood first on one foot then the other. How could you say you'd thought she was a corpse? You didn't say that sort of thing to old ladies, it was all too imminent. The eyes, pale and unfocused, stared towards him.

"Go away, lad. Don't want you here, I don't. Send Aggie oop. At once. Go on. Ought to be ashamed of yourself, you ought, doing a nasty thing like that."

Mr Blundy's fists clenched impotently. "Stupid old bitch," he said, knowing she wouldn't hear a word. He turned about and clumped down the stairs to the kitchen. "The old cow wants you," he said angrily to Ag. "Going to complain about me, she is – may as well warn you."

"Eh? What have you done now?"

"Nothing."

"Come orf it, Ernest Blundy."

"Thought she'd kicked it, I did. Felt for her heart like."

"Do ask for it, don't you. I'll go up and see to her."

Mr Blundy sat down with a sigh and took up the teacup that was waiting for him. He watched Ag fit herself into the staircase aperture and vanish, listening to the mighty creaking of the ancient woodwork as she climbed. He heard her say, "Auntie, you mustn't mind Ern," then he heard the door into the bedroom slam shut. He gloomed over his tea, shaking his head, worried sick. They couldn't hang on to Harold Barnwell for ever, and the longer they did so the greater the danger. One day the Bill would come up close – bound to. The Bill didn't like child vanishments and sooner or later they'd get co-ordinated. The essence of successful kidnap was speed – speed allied to very convincing threats. Anyway that was how Mr Blundy saw it. Let it go on too long, fail to sound blood-thirsty enough, and you gave too many chances to the Bill. In addition to all of which, you had to be fully self-confident.

Like the Loop, poor sod.

Mr Blundy, the would-be Big Blundy, was much diminished by the Loop's sad death and what was more he knew it. Fear settled on him deeper than ever as he sat drinking his tea, fear that precipitated his heart right down into his boots. He'd like to be done with all this now, turn the kid loose somewhere together with a threat of a duffing-up if ever he yacked, and then forget the whole thing.

If only he could.

Sunk in misery he heard the door upstairs open and shut again, these sounds being followed by Ag's hefty progress downwards. She loomed through the door at the bottom of the staircase, her mouth hard and her eyes staring.

"Thought she was dead, did you?"

"Yes – "

"She *is* dead and all."

It had been the most terrible shock. Mr Blundy had begun to shake like a jelly. He asked if Ag was sure. She said she was. "Dead as a doornail. Go on up and check if you want. Check your handiwork." She fixed him with a grim stare. "Gave her a heart attack you did. *Killed* her! Killed poor Auntie!"

"*I never!*"

"Feeling at her like that. Enough to kill anyone, let alone an old lady." Ag's chest heaved with emotion, real or assumed. "Lying there all still and silent she is, poor old soul. What a way to end her life, eh, have you poking and prodding like the sex fiend I said you was." She changed her approach rather suddenly. "Now we *are* up the creek. Be an inquest I shouldn't wonder."

"Not necessarily, Ag. Not if she died of the whatsit, stomach thing, there won't. 'Course, I s'pose we'll have to get the quack."

Ag agreed. "Either that or scarper. Though I s'pose we could hide the body. Hide poor Auntie." She gave a bit of a snuffle, feeling she ought.

Mr Blundy was about to sink his head helplessly in his hands when he heard a vehicle coming round the side of the cottage, then footsteps, then a banging at the back door. He shot to his feet and peered round the lifted edge of the curtain, through the window, and saw the car that had pulled off the narrow road and parked behind the barn where the Granada was garaged.

The Bill.

NINE

It was Ag who went to the door. Mr Blundy, admiring her
courage but doubting her sanity in opening up to the Bill,
lurked about in her wake feeling an urgent need to go to
the toilet. Over Ag's shoulder as she unlocked the door he
saw two figures: a slim girl in some sort of nurse's uniform,
and a cop.

It was the girl who spoke. "I expect you're the niece
and – "

"Who are you?" Ag asked, giving nothing away yet.

"I'm the district nurse."

"Oh, ah. Yes, I see."

"May I come in?" The girl smiled. "Usually I walk in, you
know. Miss Pately never locks the door."

"Ought to," Ag said. "Could be burglars and such. But
yes, dear, do come in." She was being oily now, giving
herself time to think. "What's the B— what's the police
come for?"

"My car's broken down," the girl said, still smiling, which
she wouldn't be for long, thought Mr Blundy. "Mr Parkin,
that's the constable, gave me a lift. That's all." She added
with a laugh, "He hasn't come to arrest Miss Pately if that's
what you're thinking."

"Oh my God," Mr Blundy said from the rear, reacting
naturally to the word arrest. "I should bl— I should hope
not and all – "

"Just my little joke," the girl said. Silly bitch, Mr Blundy
thought, making a joke like that. Insensitive, that, for a nurse.

The girl went on. "Miss Pately mentioned to me she had a niece and nephew living in London – "

"She did, did she?"

"Yes. Only just recently. She'd never spoken of them before. A Mr and Mrs Blundy. I telephoned a Mrs Whale – "

Ag said, "That's us." Mr Blundy caught the eye of the Bill over her shoulder and looked away fast. Ag went on, "My aunt's quite all right, thank you, nurse. I'm looking after her now, so you won't need to bother, not till we go, like."

Mr Blundy froze with sheer horror. Stupid bitch. Better to be honest about what would have to come out in the end anyway. He opened his mouth to put things right, then saw the dangers just in time. You couldn't really say Auntie was all okay when Ag spoke but now she's dead.

The nurse, however, seemed to understand perfectly. "It was more of a social call, really – she likes a visit, but in spite of the op she's really as fit as a fiddle, *wonderful* for her age. You must have seen for yourselves."

"Yes," Ag agreed. "Wonderful's the word for Auntie. Such a sweet old soul."

"Managing all on her own too," Mr Blundy said. He too had to play now.

"Yes, I know. I wish all my old ladies were as capable. Some of them are terrors."

"I'll bet," Ag said with an understanding smirk. Mr Blundy thought, why doesn't the girl push off? Ag said, "I'd ask you to step up, only she's sleeping. Seems a shame to disturb her. I'll say you called, nurse."

"Right, thanks, Mrs Blundy. How long are you staying?"

"Don't know yet. Hard to say, like."

"A week or so?"

Ag nodded. "I reckon. At least a week."

"Well, that's fine. I'll look in again this time next week and I'm always available in the meantime if I'm wanted. The op was some while back now but you do have to be careful with a gastrectomy, you know."

The nurse had turned for the door after saying goodbye, and she and the Bill were making for the patrol car and Ag was about to shut the door on them thankfully when there was a

103

tremendous crash against the door of the outside earth closet, followed by another.

The Bill stopped.

Mr Blundy virtually collapsed; Ag hissed in his ear, "*Think of something, quick.*" She pushed him out of the door, willy-nilly.

"Now what was that, sir?" the Bill asked.

"My son," Mr Blundy said with desperate inventiveness.

"Oh, have you a son?" the district nurse asked brightly. "Miss Pately didn't say anything about a son." There was another bang. "Is he all right?"

"Oh, yes, perfectly all right. It's just that he's not used to earth closets," Mr Blundy explained. "And the door jams. Just a little kid, he is. I'll see to him, don't you fret, young lady."

The girl's face crinkled into a friendly grin. "I won't embarrass him, then. Is this his first visit to the Dales?"

"Yes – "

"I'm sure he loves it, doesn't he? What's his name?"

She was only showing an interest, of course; but Mr Blundy ground his teeth, consigning her to the tortures of hell. What was his son's name? He just stopped himself saying Harold. "Damien," he came out with and God alone knew why.

"Oh, how unusual – and very nice. Well, thank you so much, both of you."

"Thank *you*," Ag said. The girl walked towards the patrol car and she and the Bill got in and backed out into the road. Mr Blundy and Ag stared at each other speechlessly for a moment, then the recriminations began.

"Stupid bitch, saying she was all right – "

"Only a moron'd say he had a son when he hadn't. S'pose they check?"

"Oh, come off it, Ag. Why should they, eh? One thing's sure since you're on about checking – they'll check your flaming Auntie, check she's not dead, one day soon."

Ag stamped her foot. "Drove me to say she was well, you did, hanging about like a wet hen and not – "

"That's right, blame me. Never think *you're* wrong, do you, eh? *My aunt's quite all right, thank you*," Mr Blundy mimicked mincingly. "God, talk about brain, some *people*!

Not all right at all, is she? But I tell you one thing: the record says she is. Says she's not only all right but is as fit as a fiddle, wonderful for her age, capable, manages for herself. Now, that makes four things – four facts that'll lead to us being nicked for certain soon as they find her, right?"

"*If* they find her."

Mr Blundy raised his eyebrows. "Eh?"

"We got to get rid of her. Dispose of her. Like I said earlier. Dispose of the body," she added in case Mr Blundy hadn't quite taken it in.

"That's daft and you know it," Mr Blundy said. "Never get away with that we wouldn't." Suddenly he stiffened. "Oh, God. Go inside, do."

"Why?"

"Big Ears," Mr Blundy hissed. "In the bog. Go in and keep your voice down."

Before following Ag into the kitchen Mr Blundy went into the earth closet and clouted Master Barnwell round those flapping lug-holes. "Just watch it," he hissed. "I'll duff you up proper, else." He hadn't removed the gag, so there'd been no opportunity for any rudeness from the kid, but the look in Harold's eye was really terrifying. A nasty mocking gleam – and absolutely no fear whatsoever. He did have guts, all right, and he'd be able to make plenty of trouble when his day of freedom came, even if they could prove that natural causes had carried off Aunt Ethel – which in itself might be difficult if the body had been disposed of in the meantime. Concealing a death was almost certainly a crime in itself, the more so when you'd done it to avoid a rap for kidnapping. "You bang again, son, and I'll bloody shove you down the bog-hole."

But in the kitchen lay the most immediate food for thought, as voiced again by Ag. They had, she said, to get rid of the body. There was no other way.

"If there isn't," Mr Blundy said angrily, "it's all your fault. If you'd said what had happened, that girl'd be laying her out now, and it'd all have been above board and honest. If – "

"Do shut up. You and your ifs." Ag loomed over him, huge and threatening and, by this time, scared as well. She knew she'd made a hash of it, Mr Blundy could see that. "What's

105

done is done. There won't be any questions asked for at least a week, so we've got that long, all right? A week to decide what we do."

"Decide where we hide Auntie."

"Yes. Couldn't leave her much longer than that anyway," Ag said. "Summer's coming."

"Get away with you, not up here it isn't. More like winter half the time."

"Maybe. Keeping's still a problem."

"I don't think that's very nice, Ag. Talking like that about your Aunt Ethel – "

"Don't you go all virtuous, Ernest Blundy."

Mr Blundy wasn't listening. He said, "Look, Ag. I say we get that nurse back, tell her the proper facts, like."

Ag shook her head. "No. It's too late."

"Yes, but facts is facts, Ag. They *are* facts, too. They'll be substantiated by a whatsit, post-mortem. Better to face that than face the – the other – "

"What other?"

"Unlawful disposal of Auntie. Concealment like. Can't you *see*?" His face appealed.

"I see one thing. A post-mortem, it'll say she died sudden. Had a shock. Now who's to say what the shock was – eh? Just you tell me that," Ag shrilled at him, hands on hips, defiance set in overweight. "Old ladies only die of shock when somebody's done something nasty to them."

"Not when they've had a gastrectomy." Mr Blundy was doing his best with the new pronunciation. He blew out his cheeks with anger and frustration. How could anyone argue sensibly with Ag? "Just because she thought I felt her tits. God, how you *twist* things. You're just being stupid. No one's ever going to say we did her in . . . *not unless we do anything with the body now*." He waved his arms at Ag, trying to penetrate her daftness. "That's where the danger is. Nowhere else."

"Just like you to argue, Ernest Blundy."

Mr Blundy made a growling noise. "All right, then, it's just like me to argue if you say so. I'll go on arguing, 'cos I'm not disposing of any body. Auntie, she's staying put. Staying in her own bed. I'm going to get that nurse girl back – "

"Don't you dare. Just don't you dare!"

"I got to do what's right."

"And that's a laugh too." Suddenly, Ag didn't look in the least like laughing. Her big, pugnacious face seemed to crumple, her lips working. She gave a big snuffle and a sort of shudder and then started crying copiously. "It's a right mess, is this. Poor Aunt Ethel. Dad's only sister. Last of me own flesh and blood she is. Was. *You* never give me none to carry on."

How unfair could you get?

After listening to a news bulletin that indicated no progress in the Harold Barnwell case, they went upstairs to pay their respects.

Auntie had died with her eyes open and Ag hadn't closed them after. She had died with her mouth open as well, being on the point of saying something or other that was now for all time lost. The result was an extraordinarily lifelike image, quite uncanny really, but the lack of movement quickly destroyed the illusion.

"Looks kind of set," Mr Blundy remarked sepulchrally.

"Peaceful, I'd call it."

Mr Blundy nodded, then scratched his head. "Wonder what it was what did it. You don't die sudden from a gastrectomy. Or I reckon you don't. Kind of creeps up on you."

"Heart attack or stroke," Ag said. "And you know who brought that on."

Mr Blundy wished he hadn't felt obliged to say something. Ag wasn't going to forget his part in this, innocent of intent as it had been. She was crying again, but Mr Blundy felt there was some crocodile element in her tears, for she had never expressed much love for the old cow.

"I'm ever so glad we were here at the last," Ag said after a moment.

"Yes, there's that. We should be thankful for that." Should they? A sight better if they'd not been. Mr Blundy cleared his throat of hypocrisy but nevertheless went on in the same vein. "Poor old soul, eh. Don't know how you can ever think of, well, upsetting her, like."

"How d'you mean, upsetting her?"

"You know."

"Disposing of the body?"

"Yes."

"Why not say so, then, 'stead of being mealy-mouthed about it? Anyway – what's the difference, I'd like to know? Bodies are bodies, aren't they? Dead. They're 'disposed' of in graves, aren't they, or cremated? It'll make no odds to Auntie now. She wouldn't want to cause trouble."

She'd caused enough already, Mr Blundy thought but didn't say so. "How about a service?" he asked instead.

"Service?"

"Church. Be bound to want that, she would,"

"How would you know?"

"Well . . . folks always do."

"Don't know so much about that. Could have been one of them atheists."

"Not in Yorkshire," Mr Blundy said with no real reason.

"Well. Offer up prayers later."

"Kind of memorial service, like?"

"Yes. But only us two to go."

Mr Blundy pursed his lips. "I reckon that'd be sort of, I don't know, sacrilegious."

She stared at him. "Why? Prayers is prayers. Before or after, comes to the same."

"Depends," Mr Blundy said slowly, almost unwillingly. "Depends on how she gets disposed of."

Ag dismissed that. She asked, "You any ideas on that, have you?"

"Shove her off of High Force, I s'pose. Or drop her down Gaping Ghyll."

"What's Gaping Ghyll?"

"Big sort of pot-hole. Long drop into a cave. Read about it somewhere. Over by Ingleborough. Sheep fall down sometimes."

"It's an idea."

"Oh no it isn't," Mr Blundy said forcefully. "Only joking, like. If you want to be done for murder, drop Auntie down Gaping Ghyll and welcome! What I read, it's around a three-mile walk from the road, all upwards. Don't be daft,

Ag. The moment we shift Auntie into the light of day, we've had it." He turned away from the death-bed and drew the curtains across the little window: Auntie had had her last sight of the mighty Pennines. He glanced across at Ag in the shadows by the bed. "Come on, then. Do the old lady up proper. It's only right."

She looked blank. "Do her up proper, what d'you mean? Lay her out?"

"No. Just close her eyes. And her mouth." Mr Blundy sounded uneasy. "Don't like the way she's looking . . . it's like she's heard."

Next day Mr Blundy took the Granada into the market town of Hawes where he bought more newspapers, seeking more detail than was provided by the radio. On the way back he stopped in Askrigg for a read; he hadn't liked to look too curious in the place of purchase – he knew this was being daft but he couldn't help it, it was almost like an act of propitiation to superstition, to primeval gods. Anyway, the read in Askrigg didn't reveal very much. There was no mention at all of the Loop: another death on the roads didn't much signify. There was a bit of a splash about Harold Barnwell, with photos of his mum and dad. The mother looked a bit of all right, the father looked a bastard – fat, hard faced and greasy with wealth. Amazing what a few old bedsteads like Auntie's could do. Anyhow: the kid had been noted missing just like the BBC had said, failing to report back to his teacher after visiting Brands Hatch. There was a large-scale hunt in progress but there still wasn't a whisper of kidnap. Mr Blundy felt confirmed in his earlier view that the Bill had no leads and were flummoxed.

Good.

There was a photograph of a detective chief superintendent – efficient, grim faced, tight lipped, framed in the window of a car. Top-ranking Bill; he looked flummoxed and all.

Mr Blundy's spirits lightened, but only for a brief moment. The basic problems remained and were very, very real: what to do with Aunt Ethel, and the kid himself. To be landed with a child and a body was certainly no joke. Shaking his head gloomily, Mr Blundy started up and drove back to Auntie's

109

cottage through more interminable Yorkshire rain. Funny that so many of the top cricketers came, or had come anyway, from Yorkshire, what with all that rain always stopping play. Rain, rain, gush, gush, down the windscreen . . .

Rain, rain. Some little jingle from childhood days. *Go to Spain*, that was it.

An idea – or not?

Not, on the whole. Unless you had your own boat, or your own aircraft, getting Auntie and the kid out of the country was just not on, frankly. Difficulty with Customs and that . . . in any case, Mr Blundy remembered, that was what the Bill always expected you to do. Once the cops cottoned on to kidnap, the ports and airfields would be soaking up an awful lot of Bill time.

On arriving back, Mr Blundy shoved the papers at Ag and she had a good, long read. At the end of it she sat and thought for a bit – cooking something up, evidently.

"I been thinking," she said at last.

"Well?"

"Auntie and that. Does seem a shame really."

Mr Blundy waited for more.

"I mean, what I suggested," Ag explained with delicacy. "Though it may have to come to that in the end. Thing is, she'll keep a week, say. And we agreed we're safe for a week – that nosey nurse girl, she won't come back for a week, we know that, and it's not likely anybody else will."

Mr Blundy stared. "Pardon me if I'm dense, like. But are you suggesting we keep Auntie for a week, and then declare her? Is that it? 'Cos – "

"Yes," Ag said with defiance.

"Stone the crows."

"*Now* what is it?"

"What is it, she asks. I'll tell you." Mr Blundy sat up straight. "How do we explain that we didn't tell the nurse the poor old soul had kicked the bucket when she came yesterday? Eh? Or do we say we just thought she was tired . . . then found out a week later she'd been dead all along, eyes and gob open an' all – "

"Shut up and listen. She didn't die yesterday, she died just

110

before that girl's next visit. Or anyway, some time between then and now. We – "

"Just a minute. How about the quacks? Can they determine a time of death, or can't they?"

" 'Course they can," she snapped back at him. "Never listen, you don't. Thing is, we haven't been here all the time. We don't *know* when she hopped the twig because we weren't here when she did. See? Just after that girl left yesterday, we had a row with Aunt Ethel and – "

"And get done for murder, motive and all – "

"Oh, shut up. She wasn't *murdered* – "

"Well, thanks a lot," Mr Blundy said tartly, being badly on edge now. "I was under the general impression, like, that you'd accused me of shocking her to death when I touched what she thought was her tit and I hadn't – "

" – she wasn't murdered, she died a natural death and that's what the quack'll say since it happens to be the truth. Now then. We had that row as I said. Auntie got in a tizz and told us to go and we went. Some days later, just under a week, say, we come back . . . to say we were sorry and to see how she was. To our utter astonishment, we found her like she is now." Ag jerked her head upwards towards the ceiling. "Dead. Well?"

Mr Blundy sent out a long, whistling breath. "I s'pose it does hang together in a sort of way, but where do we *go*? Thought of that an' all, have you?"

"The Smoke."

"London?"

"That's what I said."

"All the way back to London, all the way back up again just to say we was sorry?"

"She's me last living relative."

"Yes, but still." Mr Blundy shook his head. "It's stretching it a bit."

"All right. We wrote, got no answer and started to worry. Then we come back up to sort her out again. Come to that," she said after a pause, "we don't need to go to London, not really. Just away from here, that's all."

"Oh, for Christ's sake, where to?"

"*Don't blaspheme.* I don't know where to. Can't you ever think of anything for yourself?"

"But we can't go bloody *anywhere*," Mr Blundy said in desperation. "Not with the kid we can't. How do you take a kidnapped kid to a hotel or a bed-and-breakfast – and where else is there? Seems to me you're forgetting the whole point of all this. Auntie's only incidental really."

"I'm not forgetting anything," Ag said. "We've come this far and we don't back out. I don't want to go back to charring in Bayswater, don't you think I do. I haven't forgotten the kid. That's the whole point. When we get away from here, you put the squeeze on that Barnwell, take over where Bernie Harris left off, see?"

"But I've already told you – "

"Yes. Oh yes, you have." Ag's chest heaved with strong emotion. "You're gutless, Ernest Blundy. Go so far then get cold feet. Pull yourself together for once and aim high. Get into the big-time. Are you a man or a mouse? Do you fall at the first fence? Yes, you do, why bother to ask. Remember, he who hesitates is lost. This is where we sink or swim."

Never had so many clichés been hurled at Mr Blundy all at once. His head whirled and rattled like a fairground. He thrust it into his hands and moaned in self-pity. Ag was too much for him, too much altogether. He just couldn't hold out against her tirades when she swung into full voice. If only she would threaten to pack up and leave him he would grasp at a wonderful life-line, but she was too bloody fly for that. Her threat was to stay.

On and on, on and on again. Shout, hurl abuse – oh, it was dreadful. Mr Blundy's eardrums reverberated as though they'd been assailed by the massed bands of the Brigade of Guards plus the bagpipes.

"Stop it," he implored. "*Bloody stop it!*"

"Will you do as I say?"

"Yes," he raved, waving clenched fists in the air. "Yes, yes, *yes*!"

Peace.

TEN

The final work-out involved a compromise, arrived at after much bickering and a good fry-up for supper.

It would be risky to the point of lunacy, Mr Blundy said, to take the kid south again minus injection, and they hadn't got any more of the dope to use. Ag made the point that London was their safest bet after all because Mrs Whale would corroborate their evidence, i.e. that they were in Bass Street, Paddington, at the time Auntie had died or was said to have died. Mr Blundy pointed out that the kid couldn't be taken to Bass Street and neither, in the absence of the dope, could he live in the boot of the Granada. And he added that he wasn't in any case going down the M1, or any other road, with that thump, thump, bang, bang from the boot. Not for a fortune. Nor was he going to risk giving the kid a bash on the head to keep him silent thumpwise. He would accept the gag and the rope but nothing more.

"Aside from the risk," he explained, "I couldn't do it, never. Not in cold blood like. He's only a kid, remember."

"I know that, don't I? Ought to have kidnapped a grandad, you ought. So what, then?"

"We've decided we can't go anywhere else, not with the kid, right? And of course we can't leave him here, tied up in the bog. Starve, he would. And freeze. Can't have that."

"I ask again: *what, then?*"

Mr Blundy paused, trying to hold on to his temper. Ag was such a sneering bitch, it riled him terribly. He said, "Well, it's difficult to – "

113

"Can't you ever help? Can't you ever be more positive? Can't you – "

"Yes, I bloody can," Mr Blundy shouted with sudden truculence. "I will an' all, right now." He pointed a finger at Ag, and although it shook it remained truly aimed. "You'll bloody well stay here with the kid while I go south on me own. You'll look after him. You'll treat him well. You'll keep him hidden. You'll – "

"I – "

"You'll shut up. You'll listen to me for once." Mr Blundy felt that just one more remark from Ag would lead to real murder. He felt his head swell to bursting point. "You won't show your bloody mug out of the door, not once you won't, except to see to the kid, you won't even look out of the window. You won't answer the door. All anybody knows, you've come south with me. When I come back you come back too. Come back to life, that is. You resume living. Till then you hibernate."

Mr Blundy blew out his breath; all that had been quite an effort but it seemed to have worked. Ag was suddenly subdued, possibly from sheer astonishment. She said, "And . . . and you go to London, see to the money?"

"Yes." Mr Blundy thumped the kitchen table, hard and masterfully. Plates and cutlery rattled. "Go first thing in the morning, I will, so there."

"Well I never."

That night Mr Blundy, still on the crest of his masterful wave, once again broached the subject of sex. But this time Ag was having none of that. "Twice in, what, three days? You be satisfied with what you've had, Ernest Blundy."

"But I – "

"Said no, didn't I, and no I meant. Enough's enough." She bridled into bed and thumped down hard in the hollow. "What d'you think I am, a pin-cushion? Sex is horrid. Go away and be a sex fiend somewhere else, do."

"Mean that?"

"Yes."

Maybe he would. He fumed away to himself. When the day of wealth dawned, if ever it did now, then Ag could start

114

watching out. He'd never ever had much luck in that direction but he knew that cash drew the birds in flocks. Look at all them film stars, and pop groups, and international sportsmen and that. It was the cash that did it, stood to reason.

Come the morning, when they got up very early, the question of cash became a present as well as a future concern.

They didn't like the necessity, they told each other, but they steeled themselves and delved deep into Auntie's drawers and cupboards, and under a topsoil of intimate garments – stays and camiknickers and petticoats and such – they discovered her hoard: seventy-six out-of-circulation one-pound notes.

"Daft old – lady," Mr Blundy said in disgust. "What a bleeding waste, eh?"

But that was not the end of the haul. It was Ag who unearthed the rest: nearly a thousand quid in tens and twenties, in a shoe box.

"I better take three hundred," Mr Blundy said. "Need it, down the Smoke."

"You'll take a hundred and think yourself lucky."

"But I may have – "

"Hundred. I know you, Ernest Blundy. And don't argue, it's not right, not in this room." She added, "Have to think of the kid. Can't leave me short, see." There was something else, too. Involuntarily, she looked over her shoulder at the death-bed. "Leave that IOU you said you would."

"Don't be daft, Ag."

"It's not daft. Want to be done for murder?"

He gasped. "Eh?"

"Murder. Motive – robbery," she said. "See now, do you? Put an IOU and it's a loan before death."

"Oh, all right." Mr Blundy pulled out a biro and tore a sheet from a notebook. He wrote an undated IOU for one hundred smackers and rolled it in with the balance, which Ag shoved back beneath the camiknickers. Feeling guilty, they crept down the stairs and Ag prepared porridge for breakfast.

"Not a word to the kid," Mr Blundy said. "About the money. All right?"

Ag nodded.

115

"Or about me being away. That's important, Ag. You'll need to cover that. He's to think I've been here all the time, otherwise he could raise difficulties later. About your aunt, I mean."

"Oh? How's that?"

"How d'you mean, how's that?"

Ag's foot tapped impatiently. "Mean this, don't I: far as everyone's to know, *none* of us has been here all week. What you said yourself. That's how Auntie came to die undiscovered, innit?"

Mr Blundy's jaw sagged. Back in the daft-husband category again, and so soon after reaching the heights, it wasn't fair. "Oh, sod it," he said ungraciously.

Ag merely grunted.

"Better get off, hadn't you?" This was at breakfast.

"All right, all right."

"Sooner all this is finished, the happier I'll be. And just remember I'll be without news of what you're doing . . . so don't linger."

"No, I won't." They would be right out of communication; only the phone box in the village, and him with no known abode. Letters were out, much too risky. Mr Blundy finished his breakfast, took his leave of Ag and stole out silently past the locked door of the earth closet, carrying the small amount of personal gear he would need in London. He got into the Granada, released the handbrake, shoved the engine out of gear, got out again and pushed. The car rolled out backwards, quiet and all unheard by Master Barnwell. It went rather fast down the slope to the bumpy track and Mr Blundy, making a wild dash, just managed to leap in and control the wheel, more or less, before it crashed into the stone wall opposite. Pointed towards the A684, he drove away drenched with sweat and shaking like a leaf, drove, as had become usual, into teeming rain, heading on the long haul down the great highways for the metropolis and his destiny.

It was all up to him now – all of it.

116

ELEVEN

The motorway was horrible: it was raining nearly all the way down and there was the very hell of a lot of heavy stuff all chucking muck at Mr Blundy. He detested Long Vehicles on account of their arrogance. Also he'd seen that accusing vision again: God had manifested Himself to Mr Blundy quite soon after the Woodall service area, where he'd gone in for a cup of coffee and to top up with petrol. God had seemed to swing down from a slagheap in the middle distance to remind him of dead Auntie and suffering Harold Barnwell – as if a reminder was necessary – and of the torment he was about to bring to the Barnwell parents, indeed had already brought – though it could be that the fact of a contact would bring relief. Better, probably, to know that sonny was safe and well, even if in captivity, rather than go on wondering and letting their imaginations roam around worse fates.

God, Mr Blundy was convinced, had come down in wrath.

Of course, Mr Blundy knew inside himself that the vision came only from his own mind, that God couldn't really be there – or anyway was unlikely to be – but he had a strong belief that God had put that vision into his head and thus was, in that sense at any rate, engaged upon a manifestation personal to Mr Blundy. The implications of that were cruel. As a matter of fact the vision vanished somewhere around Leicester Forest East but was back shortly after, before Newport Pagnell.

Mr Blundy didn't read anything specific into such comings and goings, and he'd managed during the vision's absence to concentrate his mind sufficiently to evolve a plan of a sort, a plan for dealing with the Barnwell parents. As a plan it was simple and straightforward: Mr Blundy believed strongly in simplicity. It was the over-clever complications that always let you down – too much room for mistakes and the horrible quirks of chance.

Mr Blundy did not go home to Bass Street, at least not right away. He had his reasons for not going there till after dark. On leaving the motorway he proceeded along the North Circular until he turned south along the Edgware Road. Reaching Marble Arch he put the Granada in the underground car park, recalling as he did so his dad saying that the old-time London bus conductors always used to call the stop Ma Blarch.

He walked along Oxford Street, seeking a telephone box in a nice bustling area where he would be just one of the crowd currently milling about in the evening rush hour. He didn't bother to look for any on-street kiosks, they'd all have been attended to by vandals, rotten bastards. He made for the Tube station at Oxford Circus. He could have used Marble Arch, or maybe Bond Street, 'course he could, but he hadn't. Fly Blundy! Pointless to take *any* risks that weren't strictly necessary, and the more ground he put between his forthcoming phone call and his parked car the safer he felt.

At Oxford Circus he had a long wait.

There was a queue for each of the phones, or anyway at the two that were working, but at last he got his face behind one of the screens that acted as phone boxes in this day and age. He'd looked up the Haverstock number at the Toddington service area before coming off the motorway and had it written down in his notebook.

He dialled the number, feeling a shake in his fingers. The call was very quickly answered. This was natural; they'd be manning the phone day and night for news, poor sods. Mr Blundy said cautiously, "Hullo."

"Yes, dear, if you want an appointment will you ring back in half an hour, I'm about to be engaged with a client. Where did you see the card, dear?"

Bloody prozzy. And sod British Telecom too, taking his

money under false pretences, why didn't they keep their bloody equipment in better nick?

Angrily he said, "Go and get stuffed," and banged the handset down. After that he dithered. It could be an omen of failure to come. Anyway, better not to risk two calls from one box, because you never knew what the Bill might get up to. Mr Blundy brought his head out backwards, feeling immensely frustrated. Frustrated in more ways than one: even such remote contact with a woman of easy virtue had given him certain urges and ideas . . . better not, though. Business first – then perhaps he'd see. Hunching himself against a nasty drizzle as he emerged into the open, he walked towards Tottenham Court Road and tried again.

After another wait in a queue, he dialled.

He waited, shaking and shaking.

No answer.

The bastards. Gone out and didn't even have an answer-phone – didn't care, and the poor kid closeted in that bog up in Wensleydale. God, you'd think they'd have skivvies by the hundred to wait in and answer the phone. Maybe, though, there were other reasons: the Bill getting its tap on, the Barnwells not answering till they'd fetched the Bill in from the kitchen to eavesdrop. Something like that, trust the Bill.

Mr Blundy, when this thought came to him, couldn't wait to bash the phone down and scarper.

Bloody hell, the risks! And he would have to try again.

He sweated profusely. He was innately unfit for command, for high responsibility – he knew that now. He needed a lead, a guiding light – someone like the Loop. Big Blundy, his arse! He was the everlasting dogsbody, the hired hand, the taker of orders. On this sudden blinding wave of self-knowledge Mr Blundy entered a public house. Wedged at the bar, he asked for a large Scotch. Having drunk this, he felt easier: he had two more, then another.

Ah now, that was better. He would have liked more but saw that indulgence just now would be indiscreet. Make the call, *then* have another. For now he needed all his wits about him. When, the job done, he had that next drink . . . well, then he might also think about ringing a prozzy, and sucks to Ag.

119

Something to look forward to, was that, something to steel him. Deserved a bit of a reward too.

"Yes, who is it?"

Mr Blundy felt quite faint. Everything, all his prepared spiel, went right out of his mind. The answering voice was strong and harsh – in a word, authoritative. The man was a man of iron, if only scrap iron. Mr Blundy swallowed and managed to say, "Mr Barnwell?"

"Yes. Who's calling?"

"Never mind the name."

A pause, followed by a sharp intake of breath. "*What was that?*"

"I said, never mind who's calling. Want news of your kid, don't you?"

Another pause. A longish one, during which Mr Blundy saw jacks and ordinary Bill in all directions, converging on the phone, with others at the reception end of the line, all listening and deducing.

Then: "Of course I do. How, and where, is Harold, and who, and where, are you?"

Cool, eh. Mr Blundy said, "I'm not telling you all that lot, don't expect me to really, I bet. Harold's okay and that's all I'm saying. He's okay, honest he is. He's not been harmed, not been hurt in any way. He's been kept fed and warm. He's a nice kid."

"I'm aware of that. I rather like him myself. So does his mother. We like him so much we want him back – still unharmed and healthy." It was a dangerous voice, calm, collected, masterful. Echoes of the kid. "Am I to take it this is a kidnap, and you're demanding money?"

"Spot on," Mr Blundy said toughly, feeling sick.

"You know what you can do." The voice held a note of finality, of non-co-operation. Mr Blundy's flesh crept. Unfeeling bastard! The Loop could have been dead wrong – it could be that this scrap-iron merchant didn't give a fish's tit for the poor little kid, thought more about his wealth. In a high voice Mr Blundy tried to get some important points across.

"Now look," he began, and got no further.

120

"I'm not the sort of man to give in to threats. I shall see you hanged first. Everything you've been saying has been heard by the police, be very sure of that." A pause. "*Are you sure of it?*"

"No," Mr Blundy said with a burst of desperate courage, "no, I'm not. Look, you're a man of the world, I don't doubt. You know the score, no need for me to say it really. If the Bill comes in, the kid suffers, right?"

"I've already as good as said, the Bill, as you call them, are already in. Don't you read the papers?"

" 'Course I do." This was going all wrong. Mr Blundy felt the initiative slipping away as though it had been greased. "That's not what I mean and you know it, mate. I mean – "

"All right, I know what you mean. You're about to state a sum of money, you're about to announce a time and a place, you'll bring Harold, I'll bring the money in used notes, the older the better, in denominations of a hundred and under. If the police are anywhere around, *then* Harold suffers. Am I right?"

"You're a bloody marvel," Mr Blundy said ungraciously.

"Thank you. Name the sum."

"Eh?"

"*How much?*"

Mr Blundy licked at his lips. "Million nicker."

"I see. In cash, of course, as I said?"

"Yes, that's right."

"A little unwieldy, I think. You'd need a truck. And how do you propose I should raise that amount all at once? I'm only asking."

Mr Blundy gaped into the mouthpiece. Fancy asking *him*. "Bank," he said. "Or something."

"Or something. Don't be futile. Have you ever tried to raise a million pounds at short notice?"

" 'Course I bloody haven't." The bloke was worse than Ag.

"I thought probably not. I may be rich, but . . . good grief, man, why should I go on?"

"I don't know," Mr Blundy said. "Ring you again tomorrow." Then he cut the call. He shook like a pennant in a gale. He'd talked too long, been had for a sucker, tricked into not

121

ringing off earlier. The Bill would be on to him like a pack of wolves, no safety anywhere unless he scarpered fast.

He scarpered very fast indeed, almost crying in his chagrin, his disappointment and his over-riding fear. He needed a drink, but not in the pub he'd been in earlier. He found another without much difficulty. He had two more large Scotches. He didn't want to eat, he wasn't hungry. Felt sick rather than hungry, and all clammy. Also, he found that now he had no stomach for a prozzy. Too many worries, he wouldn't be able to perform and it would be a dead waste of money, and Auntie's cash hoard wouldn't last all that long, not the measly hundred Ag had let him have, the bitch, not in London at today's prices.

Better economise on the Scotch too. Mr Blundy made his way towards Bass Street, Paddington, stopping off at Marble Arch to collect the Granada. He parked the car in Bass Street – as it was dark the neighbours couldn't be sure if Ag was with him – then he let himself in. He shoved some lights on behind drawn curtains, in support – should anyone be looking, which they probably were, nosey sods – of his proposed story about them both coming home from Auntie's. He made some propagandic bangings and thumpings on the floor for the benefit of Mrs Whale, then went straight to bed.

God, the things he had to keep thinking about! There was no doubt about it, Aunt Ethel had rocked the boat good and proper by going and dying on them. It wasn't fair. Mr Blundy drew the blankets up to his chin and tried to sleep, but he couldn't, his mind was far too active. That Barnwell Senior: the more Mr Blundy thought, the more he felt sick with worry. Likely enough that conversation had been put on tape and was even now being played back, and intently listened to, in Scotland Yard. Barnwell had sounded a right sod, no thought at all for that poor little kid. There were, however, rays of possible comfort: what about the kid's mum? She'd have a say, surely?

And mums were mums. Softer than dads; looked at things quite differently and so they should. Mums were more concerned with kids than cash. Mrs Barnwell might talk her husband into a more *feeling* frame of mind.

But that still left the Bill.

The Bill could be persuasive too, in a different sort of context. The Bill would have assured the Barnwells, like they always did in such cases, that they would cope with anything the villains might do. No cash must change hands, the Bill would have said, and Harold would be perfectly all right when they leapt out from their patrol cars at Mr Blundy with their truncheons and their sharpshooters and their handcuffs and their dogs all foaming at the mouth.

What a risk it all was.

Mr Blundy didn't sleep a wink all night.

"Where's your husband gone?" Never mind what Ern had or hadn't said about leaving the kid in the bog, Ag hadn't, something she now regretted.

"Don't mind asking questions, do you? He's not gone anywhere . . . not far like. Just for newspapers. Be back soon, he will, so just you watch it."

"Why should *I* watch it?"

" 'Cos he might do you, that's why."

Harold considered the point, munching bread and cheese. "I don't think he would, you know."

"Oh?"

"He'll want to be able to say he treated me well. When the police catch him and you. He'll need a few good words said in his favour, won't he?" Harold's eyes gleamed and mocked. "By the way, how's the old lady upstairs?"

Ag started. "She's all right."

"But staying in bed?"

"Yes."

"Boring for her."

"No it's not. Got arthuritis she has."

"Arthritis, nothing to do with Arthur. I'm so sorry. Is that *all* she's got?"

"Yes," Ag said viciously. "It's *all* she's got."

"Oh. I just wondered, you see. She doesn't seem to be eating much, does she? No breakfast, no supper last night, now no lunch. I just wondered, that's all." Harold cast his eyes down, the picture of innocence. "I'd like some more ham."

"Ask proper."

"Sorry. Please."

123

"Fattening, is ham," Ag said and at once regretted it.

Harold lifted an eyebrow and remarked, "Then in that case I'd lay off it if I were you."

"Don't be cheeky." Ag raised a hand. "Want me to smack your kisser, do you?"

"Well, no, not particularly. When are you going to get in touch with my father?"

"None of your business."

"I'd have thought it was, actually. I suppose that's where your husband's gone."

"Said he'd gone for papers, didn't I?"

"Yes, you said that. I'm not sure I believe you. It's just a feeling, that's all."

Ag said angrily, "I don't tell lies."

There was a smirk. "*Don't* you?"

"Time you had that gag on again." Ag sucked in breath. Her hands were itching to give the little blighter what for, and inside her head her blood pressure was mounting. What with all the anxiety about dead Auntie, and the probable stupidity of Ern down in London, she felt she needed a vent. Master Barnwell's rudeness was the last straw. She lifted an arm and clouted his head hard. That, she could see, rocked him. They'd been too soft: now the little horror had had a taste of the other side of the coin. She said, "There's more where that came from, all right?" Then she nearly did something daft. She stared at the kid, right into his eyes, and said, "Now look. You've heard things, haven't you, no good saying you haven't. In the toilet, yesterday."

"No, I haven't heard anything." There was a cautious look in the boy's face now, a withdrawal from possible danger. "What sort of things?"

"Don't try that on me. You heard all right."

"I didn't. Honestly."

"You sure, are you?"

"Yes, I'm quite sure. Or I think I am. I may have heard something. I can't be really sure, can I, unless you tell me what things I did or didn't hear."

"If you heard," Ag said, "you'll know what I mean. If you didn't – well, you didn't. See?"

Harold stared at her, an incredulous and rude look. "No,

I'm afraid I don't. I say . . . I really don't think this conversation is getting us anywhere. Is it?"

Ag clenched her teeth together, doing her best not to clout him again in case she clouted him too hard and did him a mischief, which certainly wouldn't help matters. She said, "All right. P'raps it isn't, no. But let me tell you this, my lad: if you did hear anything . . ."

"Yes?" Harold asked politely. "Go on."

"Oh, shut up," Ag said in a high shout. She'd stopped her tongue just in the nick of time, having been about to utter threats that, had he overheard the conversation about Auntie, which, considering his questions, he very likely had, he should bear in mind that a similar fate could overtake him as well if he didn't watch out. Not that he would have believed it, probably; he'd already made the point the day before, or whenever, to Ern, that kidnappers didn't do away with their victims. But the thing was, she'd almost blurted out enough to make the kid think they had murdered Auntie, and on repetition to the Bill that could have taken on the proportions of a confession. It had been a close shave, had that. Ag picked up the gag and the blindfold, reapplied them to Harold Barnwell and then led him back to the earth-closet, securing him to the ringbolt and locking the door.

When she went back to the empty cottage, empty, that was, of all but the dead, she was assailed by an unaccustomed feeling of utter loneliness. It hadn't ever been lonely down the Smoke, London was a friendly place with all its noise and bustle and all the tourists from all over the world: Americans, Frogs, Dutch, Eye-ties, Chinks, Japs, plus, of course, terrorists, but they had never bothered her. Even the charring in Bayswater had had the bonus of bringing her in touch with people. People, that was it, not sheep and that. Her days had in fact been over-full really, what with the work, and Ern was always an anxiety, but up here in the Dales the days looked like stretching interminably and Ern was still an anxiety, the more so now for being a distant and uncontrollable one.

Should have gone herself.

Ag went to the window – sod Ern, she was taking no notice of his rubbish about hibernation – folded her arms on the sill

125

and stared out, a big red face framed in old stone. No wonder people went south when they got old, if they could afford to. Rain and mist, cold and fog. Sheep, shepherds, farmers somewhere behind the veil of weather out there, plodding about their unending tasks, wallowing in mud, dung and dale, slithering down the fellsides on their arses, most likely . . . stone the crows! They could keep the Pennines. Give her Praed Street and the good old Edgware Road any time, or if not London then Margate or Clacton or Great Yarmouth or a nice holiday camp full of jollity and people to rub shoulders with and yack about life in general when not playing bingo.

How was Ern making out?

Messing it all up, or raking in the lolly?

Fearing the worst, since the worst usually happened and she knew exactly what Ernest Blundy was like, wishing again she'd gone south herself to take charge, she yet found herself pondering on the unlikely best. Ern, she knew, wanted to get out of London. All the talk over the years about that big country house. Hot air, all of it – yet it could be within an ace of coming true. For obvious reasons of safety after the event, they wouldn't be able to remain in London – but, for her, she was decidedly against the country scene and she would put her foot down crushingly on that. Give her Rome, Paris, Berlin, Cairo, New York, Los Angeles, Rio – somewhere like that where you could really live. One day, when it had all died down, they might come back to London, not perhaps to live but as rich tourists en route from Paris to Buenos Aires (wherever that was, sounded like China). Just "stopping over" as they said in rich circles.

Ag came back to earth.

Bloody sheep.

Why, there was even sheep shit outside the back door – you stepped in it when you went to get Harold. Maybe Auntie had fed the sheep or something, like you fed stray cats down south. They were everywhere, the sheep, straying along the roads. You'd never get smelly old sheep in Paris or New York.

Sighing, Ag shoved the Calor gas oven door wide open and warmed her hands at it. She hadn't lit a coal fire in the parlour because she wasn't supposed to be here, though God alone knew how they were going to get past what the kid would say, except that it wouldn't matter a kick in the bottom what he said once they'd got the lolly, and it was best not to make any clutter or disturb the even tenor of Auntie's ways in any detail that might later be tricky to explain in relation to Auntie's death.

Ag spent the afternoon warming and pacing and thinking, and feeling she was going mad. She didn't go near Auntie: no point really and it would only depress her more. Time passed, centuries of it. Cups of tea helped, but only a little. Then supper and the temporary transference of Harold Barnwell to the kitchen. God, she even found the kid company! When Harold went back to the bog she sat on for a while then went upstairs to bed, past silent Auntie's door, which she found spooky.

The whole cottage was silent now, apart from creaks of old woodwork and, soon after she was in bed, the disappearance of silence came with the first hint of another rising wind. Sweeping down the fellsides to circle and whine around Auntie, that wind shook the cottage with a mighty force. Ag lay awake and quaked, wrapping her large body in the bedclothes as though seeking the security of the cocoon. The windows rattled, there was a hollow booming sound from somewhere and a gale swept sootily down the unused chimney. God's heaven was on the march, destroying a sinful world, and her with it – and Auntie too by the sound of it.

Ag found herself wet with sweat, thinking of Auntie. It was going to be very difficult to prove they hadn't at least assisted Auntie's departure if ever the Bill caught up with them. In the circumstances, like.

It was late the following evening, after another never-ending day of dale- and mist-hidden sheep-bleats, and Harold Barnwell, that Ag heard with terror the engine of a car pulling in round the back. There was a deathly flutter in her heart as she waited for the bang on the door that might announce the Bill and another visit from the nosey district nurse. What was she going to say this time, if they forced entry and insisted on a word with Auntie? But the bang when it came wasn't really a bang at all; it was more of a gentle tap. Sort of apologetic.

Now what?

Some nosey neighbour, or what counted as a neighbour in the Dales, about a mile away?

Ag remained stock still in the middle of the kitchen while the oil lamp flickered and cast frightening shadows around her. Another tap at the door, rather louder and more urgent this time. When she didn't open up the tapper shifted round to the window and tapped on the glass, nearly giving her a stroke. Tap, tap, tap, behind Auntie's wartime blackout material that Ag had found tucked away in a drawer of the dresser. Didn't show a chink, that didn't: Auntie hadn't wanted to draw the Nazi bombs down on the sheep.

Tap, tap, tap, tap.

Wouldn't it ever bloody stop?

Ag plugged up her ears with her fingers and plumped down heavily on a chair. Could be a ghost. Could be anything up here. Imagination ran riot: could be Auntie's spirit trying to get back in, only it wouldn't need to tap, surely, it'd just sort of swim in, right through the solid stone walls.

Not Auntie, no; she wouldn't have any business back inside.

Tentatively Ag unbunged her earholes. No more taps. Well, that was a mercy. But a moment later, a soft slither at the back door, then a slight crackle of paper . . . a note being pushed under. Ag froze. There was terror in the unknown: why should anyone want to poke a note under Auntie's door? What had she been up to in her dotage, to draw upon herself all this cloak-and-dagger business, furtive taps, notes?

The note lay there, shifting a little in the wind that howled under the door. Then the taps started again. Feeling her hair rise, Ag inched towards the note, bent down and picked it up. At first she couldn't seem to focus properly, she was in such a state. Then the words formed in her vision and smote her. The note was simple enough. It read: "Open the bloody door for Christ's sake it's me."

Ag's teeth banged hard together. Rotten bastard, giving her such jitters, typical it was. She unlocked the door and yanked it open.

Mr Blundy lurched in, gibbering.

TWELVE

"Thought you were never going to open up, I did." Mr Blundy collapsed on to a chair. "I've had a terrible time, really terrible."

"Why all the mystery, eh? Them taps and that daft note?"

Mr Blundy didn't seem to be registering. "Precautions, like. Just in case."

"Just in case of what?"

"Oh, shut up, Ag, do. I'm not fit." He said again, "I've had a terrible time."

"The Bill?"

"No, not the Bill, Ag – "

"Well, thank God for that anyway."

"Yes." Mr Blundy pulled his flask from his pocket and sucked whisky greedily.

"You won't have had time to get the money," Ag said accusingly. "Eh?"

" 'Course not."

"What d'you mean, 'course not? That's what you went down – "

"I know, I know." Mr Blundy waved his arms about. "Don't you start, Ag. Did me best."

Heavily, Ag sat down and faced him across the kitchen table. Grimness sat heavily on her face. "You'd better tell me all about it, hadn't you?" she said.

"Yes, yes, all right." Mr Blundy paused. "Not been anything on the BBC?"

"Should there be?"

"I don't know. I just asked, like. Has there?"

"No."

Mr Blundy drew his sleeve across his forehead, seeming relieved. Then he started. He told her, stumblingly and in an aggrieved tone, about his telephone call to Haverstock House, and about Mr Barnwell's sordid reaction to his demands. "Money," he said, sounding very bitter. "That's all they think about these days, is money."

"Just go on, don't bother to moralise, it don't become you."

"Well, maybe not." Mr Blundy hesitated. "Any bother this end, was there, eh? The old lady?"

Ag shook her head. "No. Only cheek from that kid, that's all. Don't change the subject. It's all got to come out sooner or later so just get on with it."

"All *right*," Mr Blundy said sulkily. "Well, that talk with the kid's dad, it was a long one. Too long, I thought after. God, I had a night and a half, I can tell you! Talk about twist and turn, I never stopped. It got on me mind, see. Thinking about it, like. He was too . . . well . . . too composed, too sure of himself. Just like the kid. What I reckoned I'd do, what I told him I'd do, was to ring again next day – today, that is. Get his answer. What I hoped was, the kid's mum would talk him round, make him see that to cough up was best for the kid, see?"

"Well?"

"Well, I didn't."

"Didn't what?"

"Didn't ring, did I?"

"Just came back up here?"

"Yes."

"Just like you an' all. No guts. No application. Start a thing and drop it – "

"I – "

" – when it gets rough – "

"I never. That's not fair – "

"You make me sick. What made you run out this time?"

"I didn't run out. I didn't ring again 'cos it was much too risky, that's why. Had to think of you, Ag. That Barnwell, he'd have had the Bill tapping the lines. Ring again and I'd

130

have been picked up right away. It wasn't safe, I tell you. Too chancy, much too chancy." Mr Blundy looked up and met Ag's eye. "Now what's the matter?"

"Matter? I'm speechless, mate! Words fail me, they do really."

"Well, I'm sorry," Mr Blundy said, more aggrieved than ever. "I had to make a spot decision, like, and I made it. As it is, we're safe. Barnwell hasn't any idea where we are, and those that do know – that copper and the nurse, they don't connect us with any kidnap. And your Aunt Ethel, she's dead. It's not that bad, why not look on the bright side?"

Mr Blundy turned it over and over when they'd gone up to bed after listening to a news summary that said the boy was still missing but made no reference to Mr Blundy's telephone call. Of course, the Bill wouldn't release that, still hoping to catch him when he rang again, good thing he'd been too crafty to risk *that*, whatever Ag might think.

The wind was blowing again, battering at the bedroom window, still intent on blowing the cottage down. Mr Blundy crouched in the lee of the rock that was Ag, sheltering against the many and varied storms of life, but the rock was an uncomfortable one, and critical.

"You got to try again, you have."

"No! I've said so a hundred times, Ag. I'm not risking it, I'm not."

"I'll do it, then. No need even to go to London. I can phone from up here somewhere."

"Oh, God, no you don't, Ag. I told you, they'll have a tap on. For crying out loud, let's keep one part of the country safe and in the clear. Look," he added, trying to sound resolute. "The money's gone, far as we're concerned. We've had it, can't you see? The Loop, he got it all wrong. That Barnwell's the wrong sort after all."

"You say that after just one phone call?"

"Yes, I do. I talked to him, didn't I? Not you. He won't shift an inch, I know that. And now the Bill, they'll know for sure it's a kidnap job. May have suspected it before, like, but now they'll know it for a fact – and like as not they've got a tape of my bleeding voice an' all."

"You've said all that," Ag snapped.

"Yes. 'Cos you keep *making* me, keeping on and on. Ask some new questions, you'll get some new answers."

"All right, Ernest Blundy: what do we do with the kid now?"

No answer to that one.

"So you're back," Harold said in the morning.

"Never been away."

"Oh?"

"Just been busy," Mr Blundy said defensively. "Missed your feeding times, like, that's why you haven't seen me around."

"I don't believe you, Blundy – "

"Mr Blundy to you. Didn't your mum and dad bring you up proper?"

That was disregarded. "I mean, I don't believe you've not been away. I bet you've been contacting my father. Haven't you?"

The question came out sharply and was accompanied by a keen look. Just like the Bill. The kid would make good Bill when he grew up.

"Now what give you that idea?" Mr Blundy asked.

"Don't kidnappers usually do that?"

Mr Blundy, to whom an idea had just come as though dropped from heaven, caught Ag's eye as she stirred the porridge on the stove, hoping to convey a message. Rubbing his hands together he said, "Why, yes, they do, come to think of it. Eh, Ag?"

Ag stared back at him but said nothing. She merely looked surprised and uncertain. Mr Blundy knew he should discuss this with her, but the idea and the moment had come up together and he felt he had to strike now. He said, "Never cottoned on, son, did you?"

"Cottoned on to what precisely?"

"Why, that we was joking." Mr Blundy laughed, throatily, heartily, loudly and unconvincingly. "Cor! We never meant to get money from your dad. We never kidnapped you. Not really *kidnapped*."

Ag and the boy stared at Mr Blundy as though he had gone

suddenly raving mad. Harold was the first to react. He asked, "What did you do, then?"

"We just wanted to have a kid, son. That's all. A little kid to have around and talk to, just like he was our own." Mr Blundy gave a propagandic sniff. "Never had one of our own, see? Wanted to give you a good time. Be pals, like. Yack about motor racing, seeing as we're both fans."

"About Nigel Mansell, I suppose."

"Yes. And Ayrton Senna."

"Now you're just sucking up."

"No, I'm not. What I said, it's the truth. Senna, he's not too bad . . . not a patch on Nigel Mansell, though – "

"Nigel Mansell couldn't catch Ayrton Senna if he was fitted with jets."

Mr Blundy spoke mildly. "Now, son, don't let's argue, eh? Let's start having that good time, why not? Spend a bit of time with us, like . . . then go home. That was the idea."

"A good time, in that earth closet?"

Something, somewhere, hadn't worked out. Harold Barnwell's eyes had grown wide with wonder and more than wonder. He said in a superior tone, "You must be even stupider than I thought, Blundy, if you think I'm likely to believe that."

"I – "

"And I'm not a little kid, thank you very much. I'm thirteen, in case you don't know."

"Now look," Mr Blundy started. "I'm – "

"Now look nothing!" Ag snapped, waving a porridgy spoon. "You're a bloody fool, so just shut up."

Mr Blundy's shoulders sagged. "All right," he said savagely, "I'm a bloody fool, now *you* have a go."

He went and sat in the car, in the shelter of the barn, bitter and hopeless. It was no good, they were all washed-up now. Stuck with the kid, stuck with Auntie's corpse, stuck in bloody Wensleydale until it all blew up in their faces and the Bill came in for the showdown. Over the wall, him and Ag both this time, and then try to start again when they were a good few years older, ten or fifteen years older. Yes, he was a bloody fool all right, a fool ever to have started this. It had been

133

too big all along, though the Loop, with his professional expertise, had made it sound easy. Come to think of it, even the Loop had probably had a small enough opinion of his capabilities – he'd given him only the guard job to do, not the brains end of it. It was the brains end he couldn't cope with, as had been proved beyond all doubt now. If only the Loop hadn't been knocked off, it would all have been different.

He was flummoxed.

Get on the run with those two encumbrances? Where was the money to come from after Auntie's nest-egg had gone? A little nicking here and there maybe. Dangerous, though. It would be too bad to go and get done for nicking a couple of quid from a till, or some tinned food from a supermarket, say, and then have all the rest come out. Ag would be no help either; she was still set on trying to raise the big money from the kid's dad. Really set on that she was, argue argue it would be from now on. And in the end, though it affected his bowels horribly even to think about it, she would very likely wear him down.

He'd been in the barn, champing his jaws and biting his nails down to the quick, for a good half-hour when Ag came out to find him.

"So that's where you are."

"So what? Can't I – "

"Been sulking, I s'pose." She leaned in through the car window. "You said, you have a go. Meaning me. Well, I been thinking."

"Oh, yes."

"Try to sound more enthusiastic. Or at least alive. We got to get out of here, Ern. We got to do that right away. There's still a bit of time left before that district nurse comes back. Give us a start, that will – "

"I don't want to move, Ag. I feel safer here."

"Not come the end of the week you won't. We can't stall that girl – "

"We can for a bit."

"But not for ever. Just once more perhaps, then she's going to get suspicious and demand to see Auntie, who's her patient, like. Oh, I know she said Auntie was wonderful and that, but these nurses, they keep an eye on old people, no good saying they don't, ever so nosey. So we get out while the going's good, and take the kid, and try again soon as we can."

"I'm not – "

"No, you're dead right you're not. Made a right mess last time. But *I am*. I'm not leaving this without a good try, so you can just get used to the idea, see?"

Mr Blundy swallowed hard and sighed. Let her think the way she wanted, it made life easier for the time being. He asked, "How about Aunt Ethel, then? Can't take her along, not possibly."

"No, we can't. I been thinking about her too. I'm against dumping her now I've thought more. That'd look like murder right away when she was found – and I reckon she would be, one day. Always are. They say you can't hide a body for ever. Shepherds and that, up here. And dogs and things."

"Well, I'm right with you on that," Mr Blundy said in heartfelt agreement, glad enough not to have to argue a point. "But what *do* we do, eh?"

"Leave her where she is," Ag said calmly.

"Don't be daft."

"It's not daft. Not daft at all. We don't want to panic. Remember, she died a natural death. That's important."

"You said – "

"I know what I said. But I also said I been thinking since. Leave the death as natural and they can't do us for that, can they? Any jiggery-pokery, like, and we're asking for it. Now, that's sense. See, do you?"

Mr Blundy scratched his head. "Up to a point, I see, yes. Still, doesn't cover why you lied to the nurse – or why we didn't report it as soon as it *did* happen, if you want to say she died after the nurse had called. Doesn't cover that, does it? Going to look funny, is that. Lead to questions, shouldn't wonder, and we don't want questions, do we?"

"That's right, put difficulties in the way."

"Got to think it out proper, that's all."

"All right," she said angrily. "You think of something, then, with your usual inventiveness."

"I can't. I admit that."

"Thanks for nothing, I'm sure."

"No need to fly off the handle, Ag." Mr Blundy was doing his best to take the steam out of the situation. There must be a solution somewhere if only they could find it, and Ag was dead right, they mustn't panic. That was rather vital, bearing in mind, difficult as it was in the circumstances, that Aunt Ethel's death really had been nothing but an act of God, timely or untimely according to which way you looked at it, and wholly natural and normal. No, they must never lose sight of that. "We'll have another good think and then see what's best, Ag."

"Better hurry, then." Ag withdrew her head from the car window and pushed open the door of the barn, half-shut by the wind. Whilst on the way out, she froze.

Mr Blundy glanced at her and then, looking past her, saw the reason for her sudden lack of activity.

A shadow was moving in the morning sun, moving long and dark towards the barn. Behind it there appeared a man: a man short and sturdy, dressed in dark clothing, a clerical collar, and something in his arms.

A bloody parson, now of all times.

The clergyman, moving on towards the back door of the cottage, became aware of Ag standing just inside the barn. He halted and gave her a grave look.

"Ah – good morning, good morning, dear lady. This poor old fellow – I found him by the side of the road. Some wretched car, no doubt."

Ag emerged from the barn, slowly.

"What is it, like?"

"Why, a badger." The clergyman seemed surprised at Ag's question. "Poor old fellow, he's in a bad way. Hit and left – simply hit and left! A townsman, of course. I feel sure that if she's fit enough Miss Pately will do her best for him. If not, he'll – "

"Miss Pately, eh."

The clergyman looked closely at Ag. "I beg your pardon," he said, "would it be rude of me to ask who you are, dear lady?"

"Miss Pately's niece. Just staying, like." *She's done it again*, Mr Blundy realised in terrible anguish. *Bloody fool!*

"Ah. Then you'll know how wonderfully good the old lady

is with sick animals," the clergyman said, looking benevolent and saintly. "Quite, quite marvellous . . . I really don't know what we would do without her. Almost two months since the operation – I hope she's keeping up the improvement?"

Invisible in the car, Mr Blundy closed his eyes and prayed: the prayer was not answered. Ag said, "She's keeping it up very nicely, thank you."

"I'm so glad. I should have called before. My parishes are *so* widespread, you know." He paused. "I wonder . . . would she care to see me now?"

"No," Ag said violently, then calmed down. "Er – sorry, Reverend. She's still asleep. Don't get up so early these days, not when me and me husband's here to help, like."

"Quite so, quite so. Then I'll leave this poor old fellow with you, and perhaps Miss Pately would look at him as soon as she's able."

" 'Course she will."

"Thank you very much. Give her my regards, won't you?" The clergyman bent and laid the badger gently on some old sacks just inside the door of the barn, raised his hat, bade Ag good morning again and departed. Ag and Mr Blundy looked at each other in silence for a moment, while fear ran like fingers of ice up and down Mr Blundy's spine. Ag was suffering too: her normally red face had turned quite white.

"All right," she said. "Don't say it, just don't say it, that's all. It was me had to do the talking, not you. I couldn't say it, not when he was standing there like the Bill, waiting to run me in."

All Mr Blundy could find to say was, "Now what do we do with the badger?"

THIRTEEN

Mr Blundy, as he wielded the spade he'd found in the barn, felt absolutely terrible about it.

The period of waiting for dark had been really dreadful.

It had been a period in which panic had grown and grown. Ag had been in a bad way after that parson's visit, realising that as a result of her own stupidity a few more days had now to intervene between her aunt's actual and theoretical deaths, an extra few days that might, when the post-mortem quacks got busy, mean extreme danger. Death due to administered shock, say, *could* still be murder after all, couldn't it?

"I don't bloody know," Mr Blundy had shouted at her. "Keep changing your mind, don't you? I s'pose it could, yes."

"We can't risk it. I tell you we can't risk it." Ag had been standing in a curiously rigid stance, over by the window, as if watching for the Bill. Her big square face had begun to crumple: it had a formless, trembly sort of look, as if she were overcome at last, largely by her own daftness. "We just can't risk it, not now we can't. But I got an idea. It was given me by that badger."

"Poor bugger's dead." The badger had died shortly after the clergyman had left.

"Yes, I know it is. Got to bury it."

"There's no need, Ag."

"Yes there is. Auntie would have done, I'm sure. I didn't know about her being wonderful with animals till that Reverend said, though I did know she was fond of them, always had

138

been. She'd have buried the badger. Now *we* bury it." Ag paused and seemed to be stiffening herself and her resolve. "And Auntie."

"*What?*" Mr Blundy leapt a mile. "What did you say?"

"You heard. Bury Auntie. After dark. In the field out the back. Not the yard. Under the badger."

"But for – "

"Don't argue, Ern, I can't stand it. It's something I got to do. Read prayers and all. She'd like to be out there, near her own cottage where she spent her life." Ag was shaking all over, like a jelly mountain. It quite unnerved Mr Blundy: he'd never seen her like this before, never in his life. "We'll do it tonight. Something I got to do, like I said, so don't argue with me, Ern."

"It's barmy. Bloody daft, if – "

"Please don't argue." Ag stamped her foot.

"We'll get done for murder sure as – "

"It's something I got to do," she repeated firmly. "It's the way out, I know it is. She won't be found, not ever she won't. Be no reason to look. We took her south with us because she was lonely. I'll ring that district nurse and tell her. She won't have any reason not to believe it. And we know Auntie died a natural death, poor Auntie, she don't want no post-mortem, all that cutting into little pieces, and interference."

It had been no use. Mr Blundy had argued on, from a deep pit of despair and terror, but he hadn't got anywhere.

Dig, dig, dig.

All rock – such barren soil, these fell farmsteads.

Only fit for sheep. Well, at least no one would be likely ever to bring a plough up here. Mr Blundy, adding a pick to the spade, poked and prodded and bashed, trying his best to keep the noise of his activity to a minimum. For once, luck was on his side: there was plenty of wind again, wind that howled and whined and shrieked and buffeted, the traditional churchyard-at-midnight background to his antics. As for Harold Barnwell, he was inside the cottage now, safe in the kitchen with Ag's transistor going at full blast. He wouldn't hear a thing, nor would he see anything. When the time came for Aunt Ethel to be brought down, Harold would be back in the bog.

139

But Harold, of course, was as ever the big imponderable: how much did that kid know about Auntie, how much had he heard in the past? Ag had reported his somewhat meaningful conversation, which could have been bravado or something, but Mr Blundy hadn't thought it wise to point things up too much by asking questions of the kid. Better, he'd decided, to leave things be.

Poke, prod, smash, dig.

Dig out the broken earth and stones and rock and pile them up beside the grave, beside the badger who was all ready to become Auntie's eternal bedmate. Mr Blundy went on digging manfully, hating his task and fearing it too. But there could be sense in it all. Ag's story did hang together. They could take all Auntie's personal things with them, clothes and whatever, and it was unlikely anyone would ever see the need to check. They could write about the lease of the cottage and even arrange for her few bits and pieces of furniture and that to be sent to an auction in Hawes. As for the grave, should anyone notice the earth disturbance, they would have the unimpeachable testimony of the Reverend that he had that morning deposited one dying badger. Come daylight Ag was going to telephone him from the kiosk in the village, sepulchrally, to say that the poor beast had died and had – at Auntie's behest, a nice touch – been given decent burial.

The trouble was, the fellsides were no more suitable for grave-digging than they were for crops. By the time he had finished, Mr Blundy was in a horrible state, what with sweat, rain and mud. And Auntie was going to have to lie fairly shallowly, though Mr Blundy had decided upon a layer of stones and rocky slabs between her and the badger. It was a lot of extra work but it was also extra security and somehow it also seemed more decent. The job done to the best of his ability, Mr Blundy went back to the barn and cleaned himself up a little in the darkness, then went over and tapped twice on the back door of the cottage. Entering when Ag opened the door, he watched the closely supervised emergence of Harold Barnwell with gag and his propulsion to the earth-closet. Once the boy had been locked in, Ag returned and Mr Blundy felt his stomach reacting to thoughts of Part Two of the operation, now imminent.

140

"All ready?" Ag asked.

"S'pose so."

"Come on up, then." Ag seized the oil lamp.

Mr Blundy creaked up the steep, narrow stairs behind Ag, his very guts seeming to melt away. Inside the bedroom Ag's lamp flickered eerily on death. Everything about the room seemed different from the last time he'd spoken to Auntie in her bed. A sort of stillness and silence that was never quite so total in life. Mr Blundy gave himself a shake.

"Now what's the matter, eh?"

"Nothing, Ag. Just I don't like it, that's all."

"No more do I. Sooner it'd been in a churchyard I do admit. But I don't reckon Auntie'd worry."

"Always been on the Godly side you have, Ag. Till now. I don't understand you."

Ag shrugged. "Mourn her in me own way, I will. What's mourning anyway? Self-pity, that's what it is. Ought to look on death as a wonderful thing, that's if you believe in what you say in church, like. For them as is dead, I mean. Peace and light, like, see, no more worries about gas bills and that. If your belief is *real*." She took up a position on the west end of the corpse, the feet end. "Strip off the blankets."

Mr Blundy did so, shuddering.

"Now give her a lift up, head end. That's it. Now swing her."

Mr Blundy stumbled backwards towards the door, portering the head. Auntie sagged a little in the middle: rigor mortis had long since come and gone again and she was pliable. It seemed like Ag meant to have her go down the stairs head first, which was irreverent and awkward. Mr Blundy, going down with extreme difficulty, thrust his elbows out sideways to the walls to help take the strain by friction. At the bottom he nearly fell flat on his back, but just managed to keep his equilibrium and his grip on the dead.

"Careful!"

"Being careful as I can, aren't I?"

"Aren't I, well, that's rich." Ag gave a horrible laugh and Mr Blundy realised he had inadvertently made a sort of pun. He looked wide-eyed at Ag; such a thing to say, he was really shocked, couldn't make her out at all. But maybe it was like quacks and nurses: you had to make a joke of the horrors or you'd go barmy in no time. Same with professional undertakers, probably. Mr Blundy still thought it was in poor taste all the same. He carried his end of the body towards the back door, taking the weight on one knee and standing like a stork while he fumbled the door open and held down Auntie's nightdress against a gust of wind. Then out into the dark, windswept yard, past Harold Barnwell in the toilet and up towards the low dry-stone wall between yard and field. Auntie was hefted over to lie for a moment on the ground in the wall's lee while Mr Blundy and Ag got their breath back.

"Where's the grave, eh?"

"You nearly got one foot in it," Mr Blundy panted. Ag, peering down, moved swiftly but clumsily backwards and put a foot on the body of the badger, giving a high scream.

Savagely Mr Blundy said, "Shut up."

"Should have brought a light."

"Don't be daft." Mr Blundy bent and laid hands on Aunt Ethel. "Come on, then, give us a hand."

"No, wait."

"*Now* what?" Mr Blundy straightened.

Ag said, "We should have dressed her, Ern. Not just a nightie, it's not right. She'd never have gone out of doors in a nightie." The wind blew around the graveside, tugging and buffeting. "Cold, too. Cold for – "

"Tell you something else it is an' all."

"What?"

"It's too late."

"I can go back – "

"Oh no you bloody can't," Mr Blundy said with menace. "I can't stand any more of this. Let's get it over. She won't worry what she's wearing, not now she won't."

"But it's not decent, Ern."

"More decent than me pulling off her nightie," Mr Blundy said with belligerence. "She's not going in dressed and that's that. Now give me a hand and shut up." Once again, he bent; so, this time, did Ag. The body was lifted, moved sideways, lowered into the grave. Mr Blundy, shaking and feeling really sick, was much on edge. "Now the prayers," he said, "quick, before I fill it in and add the badger."

142

"All right."

Far above, the high peaks of the lonely Pennines, invisible yet very present, frowned down below the storm-dark northern sky. The wind was blowing louder, howling and bustling about the fellside. From somewhere lower down in the dale there came the storm-tossed moo of a solitary cow.

Ag began.

A mumbled Lord's Prayer and then, for no apparent reason, Gentle Jesus Meek and Mild; after that what Mr Blundy took to be the Jubilate, more or less.

Praying done, Mr Blundy unclasped his hands and unbent his neck. He took up the spade.

"Cheerio, Auntie," Ag said through sudden tears.

Mr Blundy dug deep into his pile of stony earth.

"Earth to earth," said Ag.

"Look out for the bloody badger, do," Mr Blundy said suddenly. The animal had rolled into the grave before time; Mr Blundy removed it and carried on filling in, eventually putting on the rock and stone slab layer. On top of this he placed the badger and then completed the job, a difficult one in the almost total dark. When the shared grave was filled he flattened down the earth with the spade, then shoved some surface rocks about so that the patch looked, or anyway he hoped it looked, nicely camouflaged.

"Amen," he said simply and reverently but belatedly. "Now let's get away as fast as we bloody can."

Mr Blundy unlocked the earth closet and, reaching in, removed the gag.

"Come on out, son," he said, unhooking Harold from the ringbolt.

"It's not breakfast time, is it? It's still dark."

"I know it's still dark. We're moving out."

"I see. Have you heard from my father?"

"No."

"Oh. Where are we going?"

"Never you mind about that. Just come out. And be a good boy, mind."

Harold blinked in the light from the oil lamp that Mr Blundy

143

was holding. "What, in your view, does being a good boy involve?"

Mr Blundy hesitated. He fancied the time had come to reveal some of the truth and also ask for a bit of co-operation. "Look, son. Things have gone a bit wrong – "

"I thought they might. I do know my own father, you know."

Superior little sod. "Yes, 'course you do. Thing is, what do we do with you now, eh?"

"You tell me. You're the kidnapper, aren't you?"

Mr Blundy compressed his lips. "There's two alternatives. One: dispose of you, like. You know what I mean by that. There's plenty of ways, plenty of places around here. Or two: we take you near your home and let you go. Trouble is, if we do that, you'll talk, won't you? About us, I mean."

Harold seemed to consider the point. He said, "Yes, I suppose I might. But then again I might not. Of course, I can't deny the actual facts, can I? I mean, I can't say I wasn't kidnapped. You've already been in touch with my father – I know that, because the fat woman has rather a loud voice, hasn't she? It must be dreadful for you, living with that. As a matter of fact, I wasn't quite sure until just now, but you've just confirmed what I thought I heard by saying you hadn't heard from my father. Do you follow?"

"Bloody little perisher."

"Yes, I probably am. However, you do see the point? Since you've already been in touch with my father, I can't deny the kidnap." Harold's eyes gleamed in the guttering light. "I can say I've no idea where I was taken, though. I can be positive about that if you like. I've never heard of Windersett. The same about you and the fat woman. I don't know your name's Blundy, Ernest Blundy. Or that the fat woman is Ag. I don't know anything about Bass Street, Paddington. Or about Mrs Whale."

Mr Blundy sucked in a horrified breath. This was appalling, they were done for. He said threateningly, "Taking a big risk, you are! With you knowing all that lot, why, you're not safe to leave around, you aren't. I could duff you up, couldn't I, sew you up."

Harold smiled. "Yes. I don't think you will, though."

144

"Just tell me why not."

"Sewing anyone up is murder, isn't it? Or was when you were young."

"Now look here – "

"That's why you won't do it. You and the fat woman are not murderers – I've made that point before, if you remember. Besides, they don't like child-killers, inside. They duff them up, don't they?"

Such innocent eyes. So much guile, too much altogether for a kid. Mr Blundy was speechless. Harold Barnwell was not. He went on, "I won't say anything about the other woman either, the old one. Aunt Ethel, isn't she? Miss Ethel Pately. I believe you've murdered her, though I'm not sure. I – "

Mr Blundy pounced. "You said we wasn't murderers."

Harold considered the point. He'd been shaken, Mr Blundy could see that, he'd committed a stupid indiscretion, he wasn't as clever as he seemed to think he was. But the kid, give the little sod his due, got out of it neatly. "I take back murder. You caused her to die. She was probably honest and tumbled what you were doing, and the terrible shock killed her."

Not quite spot on, but near enough to be alarming. Mr Blundy's heart missed several beats and he felt faint and ill. One thing, the kid wasn't too certain of his facts about Auntie, by his own admission, that was . . . but there was quite enough danger around as it was.

Something had to be done.

Mr Blundy began to wheedle.

"You won't talk about all that, will you, son? We've treated you all right, you know we have. Fed you proper, haven't harmed you in any way at all, we haven't. Could have been different, couldn't we?"

"Oh yes. I'm taking all that into account." Harold watched him, shivering in the cold wind that swirled into the earth closet. "Can't we continue this conversation indoors, please?"

"Yes – yes, 'course we can, son. Come along in." Mr Blundy put a protective arm around Harold's shoulders and helped him off the seat. He led him indoors, wrists still bound behind his back, into the nice oven-warmed kitchen where Ag was waiting and showing impatience.

145

"Well?" she demanded.

"Get him a nice hot drink, eh?"

"Now look – "

"Shut up and get it, Ag." Mr Blundy signalled over the boy's head by means of a contorted wink. "He's cold and upset, like."

"I'm not upset," Harold said calmly. "I'm going home, aren't I?"

"Maybe, son. Depends, don't it?"

"But there's still the question of how much I'm going to remember, isn't there?"

"Yes."

"There'll be a lot of questions."

"Yes."

"My father and the police. It won't be very easy."

"No. But you'll manage, I know you will – eh, Ag?"

"There's more behind him than meets the eye," Ag said.

Mr Blundy moved round the boy and looked into his face. "Is there, son?"

"You bet there is," Harold said, grinning. Noting the grin, Mr Blundy's heart sank. Little sod, his teachers would be dead sorry to see him back. Talk about crafty! Mr Blundy's mind was getting there now, fast. Harold Barnwell continued, "For not saying anything about you two, for not even remembering Windersett or Aunt Ethel or anything like that, I'll want a hundred quid a week, payable monthly in advance. My father doesn't give me very much pocket money and I find Brands Hatch expensive. Also I like to get to Silverstone for the Grand Prix. And I'm saving up to buy a racing car when I'm old enough to drive. Well?"

"You little sod!" Ag and Mr Blundy said together. "That's blackmail," Mr Blundy added.

Harold gave an almost cherubic smile. "Yes, it is, isn't it? I'd like your answer before we get to London."

Ag aimed a clout at his head. "Little beast," she said viciously. "You'll not get away with extortion, you won't. London, my foot! There may be another sort of destination for you, one that'll shut your big mouth better than cash. If I were you, I'd be thinking about *that*."

Harold gave one of his superior smiles and turned to

146

Mr Blundy. "That fat woman's awf'lly dense, isn't she? I'm offering her the only safe way out and she hints at *malum in se*."

"What's that?"

"*Malum in se*. Wrongdoing – in Latin. Jiggery-pokery. Awf'lly stupid. I repeat, both the police and the villains absolutely loathe and detest child-murderers. You'll have a simply terrible time in the Moor and Holloway respectively. Surely it's worth a hundred a week to avoid all that, isn't it?"

Mr Blundy met Ag's eye. "Twenty," he said sourly, though God knew where it was going to come from.

"I'll settle for seventy-five."

"Twenty-five."

"Fifty."

In the end they compromised on thirty. Little bastard, rotten little blackmailer! Mr Blundy's hands, almost involuntarily, moved towards the lovely target of Harold's skinny neck. One squeeze, one quick flick, and a lot of cash he hadn't got would be saved. God, it was tempting! But Mr Blundy resisted the temptation. The kid was only too right. Mr Blundy, who had absolutely no faith in his own ability to get away with actual murder, knew that the dangerous cons in the Moor, or the Ville, or Parkhurst, would certainly make the Loop's duffers-up look like Boy Scouts at a garden fête. His hands relaxing, Mr Blundy retreated from suicide – yes, you could be really sewn up inside, he'd known it happen and always in such a way that it looked like something else, the best cons being far from stupid.

"Bring the money on the second Sunday in each month," Harold said, scenting victory. "That's our day for meeting our parents or other relatives. We're allowed down into the town. Be outside the gates at 2.30 p.m. You can be an uncle from Australia if anyone asks."

"Why Australia?"

"To account for your Cockney accent."

"Oh, I see. And how, may I ask, are you going to account for having so much bloody cash, eh?"

"My father," Harold said calmly, "has a very good accountant who handles all his business, including my own funds. And I happen to know the accountant is having an affair with my

147

mother and he knows that I know. Payment in advance to cover the holidays. And if ever you don't turn up, my memory comes *straight back*."

By the time they were all ready to move out the wind had dropped and the dawn had come: a lovely dawn too, bright and clear and fresh, with streaks of green and pink and purple spreading from the rays of the rising sun to touch the Pennine peaks and then bathe the dale in heart-warming splendour, just like any day when after a wet holiday you were home-ward bound. Sheep woke up and gambolled with their lambs, farmers rose from their beds to muck out byres, birds sang, some early heavy traffic rumbled along the A684, bound for Kendal and the Lakes or the other way for Northallerton and the North Yorkshire moors beyond the Hambleton hills. The squat man who was crouched behind the old Granada in the barn, the man with the gun and the cushion which he would use as a makeshift silencer if necessary, shivered in that cold northern dawn and looked again at his watch.

Any minute now.

Blundy wasn't going to get away with it whatever it might be he was trying on.

Blundy was due for the chop if he'd been trying any funny business, any double-dealing or such.

FOURTEEN

"Am I going in the boot again?"

"Yes," Mr Blundy said. "For safety's sake, see – don't want to get done by any Bill when I'm on my way to hand you back, like. That's natural, you'll agree."

"Yes, of course."

"And don't you bang and thump."

Harold shook his head. "All right, I won't. Just a small one when I want you to open up for anything. Don't forget the blankets and pillows."

"I know my job without you telling me."

"I just wondered."

"Well, stop wondering and shut your gob before I lose my temper and duff you up."

"That stupid expression again."

Mr Blundy lifted a hand and aimed a half-hearted cuff that missed. "Ag," he shouted up the stairs. "Ready, are you?"

"Keep your hair on, I'm coming, aren't I?" There was some heavy motion overhead and half a minute later Ag came down with her bag packed, just as though she'd been up to thank Aunt Ethel for having them. Also with her was a suit-case of Auntie's, complete with such clothing as Auntie would be presumed to need on a visit south; and in her handbag was the balance of Auntie's cash together with Mr Blundy's IOU. Ag glanced around the kitchen with a professional house-wife's eye. The place was to be left neat and clean, just like Auntie would leave it when going away to stay with her niece and nephew-in-law. Nothing must be overlooked, nothing.

149

"Hurry up," Mr Blundy implored. He couldn't wait to be away now, away from Windersett, away from Yorkshire. Away from the proximity of Auntie.

"Calm yourself, do," Ag said, making for the front parlour. She was back inside the minute, having had a good look around a room that in fact had not been used since their arrival. "*Now* I'm ready. Just check the toilet on the way out." She went to the next door. Mr Blundy and Harold followed her through and the door was shut and locked for the last time. Ag put the key in her handbag. She looked into the earth closet, announced that all was well, then shut and locked that door too.

She led the way to the barn and was first in, thus was the first to encounter the squat figure that emerged from behind the Granada.

She screamed.

"Hold it," the squat man ordered. "No noise, right?"

"What's up?" Mr Blundy called, coming in behind Harold Barnwell. "Oh, my God. Oh, Christ! The bloody Bill. Oh, God."

"Bill, nothing," the squat man said, spitting on the ground. He came closer, bringing his gun. It looked very steady and he looked very capable of using it. "Don't worry about the Bill, the Bill's too busy going through the bookshops for porn. Me, I'm a mate of the Loop's. And why, you may ask, am I here in bloody Windersett? Three guesses."

"Come for the kid," Mr Blundy mumbled. He didn't recognise the man.

"Right first go." The gun-hand nudged closer to Ag. "Didn't imagine, did you, the Loop'd leave real business to you? Now the Loop's done for . . . that's where I come in, like. See?"

"Just where do you come in, eh?"

The squat man grinned briefly. "Call it collection agency. As of now I'm – "

"Mean you get the ransom money, do you?"

"Just said so in effect, didn't I?"

"You been in from the start, like?"

"I have, yes, d'you mind? This is big, *too* big for the likes of you. You were just the dog-handler."

"Dog-handler?" Mr Blundy was in a complete daze now, and entirely unsure as to how and where he stood.

"You know what I mean." The newcomer inclined his head towards Harold Barnwell. "The Loop – "

"I don't believe you," Mr Blundy said, having gathered together a little courage. "I was to get a half cut and you don't give half cuts to – "

"Half cut, now that's a laugh. You'd have been so lucky." The gun moved closer – closer to Ag, who looked like being the lead absorber if the gunman was given cause for alarm. "Where were you lot going? I didn't reckon on you all coming out in a bunch, looking like you was going on a journey. Come on, I want to know. Thinking of collecting, were you?"

"No. Going to hand the kid back," Mr Blundy growled. "Proper little pest an' all. It'd all gone wrong anyhow."

"How's that?"

"You don't know? Nothing in the papers, like?"

"What should there have been, beyond what I read, which wasn't much?" The voice was hard and dangerous now; so were the eyes – very. "What you been up to?"

Mr Blundy swallowed. The Bill was evidently being canny, still giving nothing out about his phone call to Barnwell Senior. He told the squat man the facts, feeling he had no option with the gun a matter of inches from Ag's gut; naturally, he made no mention of Auntie. "I didn't fancy going on, considering the risk of a trap after the first call," he finished, "so I come back up here. After that, well, I reckoned it was too late, like."

The gunman nodded and looked more or less satisfied. "Gutless bugger, aren't you, but that's no skin off of my nose, is it? Fortunate really – for you as well as me. If you'd gone and collected I'd have had to see to you, wouldn't I? So there's always a silver lining, right?"

"Right." Mr Blundy agreed whole-heartedly with the particular point made: he certainly would not have wanted to be seen to.

"So just all three of you move back into the open," the gunman said. "You and your lady wife, you keep out of it from now on. You just stand back. Do nothing till we've

gone – don't move out till we've been gone fifteen minutes
– say nothing after. Not to the Bill nor any sod else. Take
my advice and get right away from here – back to the Smoke.
And remember: one tiny little word to the Old Bill and you
might just as well jump off of the dome of St Paul's. You."
He prodded the gun muzzle right into Ag. "Got an aunt.
I know that 'cos the Loop said so. How much does she
know, eh?"

"Nothing," Ag said promptly.

"Sure?"

"Would we have told her anything? It was our necks, wasn't
it? Not Auntie's."

The gunman grinned again. "That's right. Still is. So watch
it, all right? Now – move."

They moved, all of them, shuffling out backwards into the
yard near the earth closet.

"Kid comes with me. I got a car down the track. Also two
mates with guns. Don't try anything. Just remember you've
already kissed the cash goodbye as of your own free will, so
you're no worse off. 'Cept you've lost the kid."

"Little perisher," Mr Blundy said half-heartedly. The kid
hadn't been all that bad, not really – sharp-tongued and
rude but then Ag really *was* a fat woman and he'd had his
points. "Well – goodbye, son. Sorry about all this. Not my
fault really. Force majeweer, see."

Harold's face was white and he looked close to tears. The
squat man was all too plainly a very different kettle of fish
from Mr Blundy who, for one thing, had never carried a
gun. Cuffs and clouts and earth closets were comparatively
harmless.

"I don't want to go with this man," he said. "I'd rather stay
with you if you wouldn't mind."

"Jesus, son, I'm sorry," Mr Blundy said, sweating. "I really
am sorry, but what can I do about it, eh?"

"Bloody crying he was," Mr Blundy said savagely, jerking at
his gears when the fifteen minutes were up. In his mind's eye
he could still see the small, anguished figure making its forlorn
way down to the track ahead of the now concealed gun. A
few minutes after that he and Ag had heard a car start up

and move away. That was when he'd become all sentimental. "Poor little bugger, trusted us and all."

"Trusted." Ag gave a snort. "If you ask me, we've come off better'n we might have done."

"How?"

"Obvious, innit? No blackmail."

"Well – yes, there's that." Mr Blundy sounded a shade more cheerful but at the same time doubtful. "There's still Auntie, remember."

"I've not forgotten. Stop at the first phone box you come across."

"What for, Ag?"

"Pity *you* can't remember things, Ernest Blundy. Ring that district nurse about Auntie, ring the Reverend about the badger. Phone book'll say who the local Reverend is."

A slight delay over the call to the rectory: three bum shots before success, since they didn't know which parish actually housed the communal incumbent: a man washing down the yard in the Wensleydale Heifer public house in West Witton eventually sorted that one out for them. Mr Blundy and Ag drove on fast for Leyburn, not taking the Ripon road this time but continuing on to pick up the A1 just beyond Bedale, whence in due course they would hit the M18 and then the M1. London beckoned now, more or less. At least in London safety lay, for they would be inconspicuous and the squat man and his mates certainly wouldn't be doing any grassing on them since they had a very nice bag of beans to spill. With any luck at all, always supposing nothing went badly wrong over Aunt Ethel, they were going to be okay. Penniless, but okay. It had all been a waste of time, as Mr Blundy moaned continually, but no worse than that.

"Or *maybe* no worse," Mr Blundy added to his twentieth moan, having just been struck by a thought.

"Why maybe?" Ag asked.

"Well, look at it. When the kid gets back to his old man, after the ransom's been paid, see, he's going to come out with our part in it, isn't he? Now he can't blackmail us, like." Mr Blundy, from whom until now this aspect had been mercifully hidden, grew more and more agitated about it. "I mean to say, he's bound to. Though we *did* treat him right – he'll say that, I should think. Could count, but I dunno. It's a worry, Ag."

"Stop thinking about it and moaning."

"Well, I like that! How can I help it? Thinking of you too, aren't I?"

"I don't believe we need worry about what the kid might say. Not worry at all."

Mr Blundy didn't much like her tone; he found something ominous in it, or anyway something nasty. "Why's that?" he asked as he overtook a Long Vehicle.

"Didn't like the look of that man, I didn't."

"Nor me neither, Ag, but – "

"Different from us, like."

"Yes."

"Well then."

"How d'you mean?"

"Use your loaf."

Mr Blundy suddenly felt quite sick. "You mean . . . you really think . . ."

"*Yes.*"

"Oh, no. Poor little so-and-so. Can't be, Ag. Not that!"

Ag shrugged. "Not our fault."

"Yes, it *is* our fault. We hooked him off from Brands, didn't we? God, I'll never be able to face Brands again, I won't. I'll see that poor little kid everywhere, I will, paddock, stands, Druids, Top Straight. He *loved* motor racing, bloody loved it. Going to spend his blackmail money on it an' all."

"Exactly," Ag said in a tart tone.

Mr Blundy gave a sound like a groan. "How can you talk like that, Ag? No feelings, have you?"

"He *was* going to blackmail us, remember?"

"Yes, but that was natural – "

"Natural, my arse," Ag hooted at him. "Don't you go and take leave of what senses you got left, Ernest Blundy. Look facts in the face and shed no tears over them what has too many eyes to the main chance. It was him or us, you know that, don't you? Him or us. Well, we're us and we're going to be all right."

154

"And let that rotten sod go and kill the kid once he's got his dirty hands on the cash?"

"I don't *like* it any more than what you do," Ag said patiently, "but that's *life*, innit?"

Mr Blundy was all shaky inside, in a right mental state, but on the wheel his hands were steady steel, his foot on the gas inexorably pressing. Long Vehicle after Long Vehicle loomed up ahead, and was gone in his slipstream. The old car was going fine today; it had always liked long runs and good, keen air, responding much better to that than it did to the high summer days, the hot days and the stop-start racket of fumy London. Mr Blundy shot past not only Long Vehicles with their great trailers loaded with all manner of merchandise and their oily, mucky exhausts, but also Volvos and Bentleys and Rolls-Royces, even a Jag or two and a grinning-arsed Japanese abortion. Things were formulating in that disturbed mind of Mr Blundy's. Or anyway, beginning to – he hadn't got far yet. But his thoughts were with the kid, that trusting little kid who hadn't wanted to be snatched away, cruelly removed from Mr Blundy's gentler kidnap. God, it was dreadful just to think about it, to think of the murderer's hand getting closer – for by this time Mr Blundy had managed to convince himself that Ag had been absolutely right and the end was at hand for Harold Barnwell. And he couldn't bear, simply couldn't bear, to have that on his conscience for the rest of his life. If he, Ernest Blundy, hadn't gone along with the Loop – whose death had no doubt been due to a rubbing-out by Providence for his sins – then the poor little kid would have been okay, learning his Latin and whatever, and his Shakespeare, and peacefully, if that was the word, attending the uproar at Brands and Silverstone. It was rotten, to go and do all this to a fellow fan. Of course, if he, Ernest Blundy, *hadn't* gone along with the Loop's schemes, then maybe someone else – the squat man probably – would have done; but that wasn't the point and Mr Blundy wasn't going to allow himself to skate out from his responsibility that easy way. The facts were plain enough: he, Ernest Montgomery Blundy, had been the one who'd gone and done it.

Nor did he lose sight of another fact: he and Ag, they

could possibly be considered as accessories before the fact or something. Most likely would be. And that made them killers too, if the kid died, didn't it, in the eyes of the law?

Mr Blundy sweated profusely.

What could he do?

Nothing.

Well – not quite nothing. He could go straight to the Bill and tell them the facts, thus saving the kid's life if the Bill got on the move fast enough. He could describe the squat man, if not the car, he could tell them where the Loop had hung out, he could tell them the names of some of the Loop's pals. The risk to himself was all too obvious, and to Ag as well, of course – for one thing, it could come out about Auntie up there in the wilds in her makeshift grave with the badger – but Mr Blundy was almost past caring now, and of course they hadn't *killed* Auntie, just buried her.

He had to save the kid, do anything he could to help – and in any case he no longer shared Ag's optimism as to the nice, safe outcome awaiting themselves in London. Taking this thing at its lowest level, a confession in time to save the kid would go very nicely in his favour. What with that and the good, decent treatment he'd accorded the kid, wasn't it obvious?

It was an' all.

Well, then!

But not a word to Ag.

Things had not gone well with the squat man. Harold Barnwell was a pain in the neck, full of complaints and moans until the squat man stopped the car and lectured him and got one of the gunmen to give him a smack in the kisser to shut him up. After that there had been trouble with the car, symptoms of unrest in the innards, like dirty petrol or maybe the petrol pump was on the blink which would be serious. Anyway, the engine was losing power and the squat man pulled into a lay-by for a look-see under the bonnet. He didn't exactly find anything but he tweaked at a few connections, tightened up here and there, and when he started up again things seemed to have improved, but every now and again thereafter the engine played up and had to be looked at again, but after a while it improved. It lost him some time, though, which meant more time spent with Harold Barnwell, and later a stop so the kid could relieve himself, well guarded, behind a hedge.

Ag, like Master Barnwell, needed relief. On the M1, Woodall loomed and Mr Blundy took the Granada into the slip road for the service area. While Ag absented herself, he looked around for the Bill, but the Bill wasn't there. He took the opportunity to fill up with petrol; then, with things still gelling in his head, he came to a sudden momentous decision: he would be sure to find a police presence in one or other of the service areas on the way south, and when he did, Ag would be a problem. Better to do what he had to do without the encumbrance of Ag.

Much better.

He drove straight out from the petrol pumps, back on to the M1. Someone, taking pity on Ag's predicament when she emerged from the Ladies', would give her a lift down to London. Just before Mr Blundy entered the access road for the motorway, his eye was caught by a girl, a girl waiting for a lift. The girl was well built, her skirt was short and there was no Ag.

Why not?

It was a temptation, no denying that. But Mr Blundy had more weighty things to do and the presence of a bird might look bad to the Bill. In any case, the kid's welfare was now paramount. Mr Blundy stifled his other feelings and drove on past.

Something like a halo settled on his head, figuratively. And that reminded him of the curious presence of God when last he'd been on the M1. God wasn't here today, and what with Auntie and all, you'd have thought He would be, really. On that last trip south, when Mr Blundy had gone on his abortive trip to contact Barnwell Senior, the vision had come at Woodall or thereabouts. Perhaps absence was a hopeful sign, a sign of approval for what Mr Blundy was going to do for the kid . . .

Mr Blundy drove fast. This thing had to be done quickly; got over, in case his resolution failed. Thinking – just thinking – of resolution did something funny: it gave Mr Blundy second thoughts.

Why stick his neck out?

An anonymous telephone tip-off could do the trick. Why had he not thought of that before?

Just the ticket.

Soon after this, the next service area came up and Mr Blundy once again entered the slip road and parked the Granada. Here the Bill was in evidence, a patrol car parked outside a sort of hut. But, in obedience to his new resolution, Mr Blundy made for the telephones inside the main building, outside the cafeteria.

He was about to enter when he saw something, something that stopped him dead, shook him rigid with its total unexpectedness.

The squat man, getting into a car. A Volvo, it was. No sign of the kid; he'd most likely be in the boot. There was no doubt about the squat man, who'd been getting petrol and hadn't seen Mr Blundy.

What now?

The telephone, or the Bill direct? The Volvo was moving off and the Bill would take all day, checking Mr Blundy's story and letting the squat man get away with the kid. Same if he used the telephone.

It was all up to himself now. Mr Blundy felt a rush of blood to the head, a surge of unaccustomed bravery. He flew back to the Granada, got behind the wheel and drove fast for the access road and the motorway, not far behind the Volvo. He pressed the accelerator almost to the floorboards. He was going to stop that Volvo if it was the last thing he ever did, cut in and force the squat man on to the hard shoulder, force him to stop, and then what? Wave down a passing car and get the driver to use one of the emergency phones to bring the Bill in pronto.

Driving at breakneck speed, Mr Blundy took the Granada into the fast lane without using his rear-view mirror. A horn blasted at him and he veered back to the centre lane and another horn blast. Headlamps began flashing from behind, where there was a fair degree of chaos. There was also a police car, in the middle lane; its crew might come in very handy.

Mr Blundy pressed on. He was bathed in a nasty, sticky,

cold sweat. He had to use his judgment; he mustn't harm the kid. That was the first consideration. But just the same he had to stop the squat man who might in the end harm him a bloody sight more.

He swept past the Volvo. He was pretty sure he hadn't been recognised but the squat man pulled into the fast lane right behind him as though he wanted to nudge him out of the way. Naturally, with the Bill not far behind, the squat man wouldn't risk passing on the inside and maybe get flagged down. Not with the kid in the boot.

Mr Blundy thought like lightning and did what he knew he had to: he slammed on his brakes and turned very slightly towards the safety barrier. In the split second that followed, Mr Blundy, this time using his rear-view mirror, saw the reaction in the squat man's face and then there was a dreadful, tearing crunch as the squat man gave his wheel a jerk left and in the process of trying to zoom past took Mr Blundy's near-side rear bumper and hefted him on to the safety barrier.

It was fairly spectacular.

Seventy-eight crashes down all three southbound lanes, a number of vehicles written off and a number of injuries. Miraculously no deaths except Mr Blundy. Harold Barnwell, who had as expected been in the Volvo's big boot, had been bundled in rugs and blankets and pillows but was badly shaken up in the car's spin down the centre lane and its final lifting on to its side. However, apart from that and a cleanly broken arm he was unhurt. The boot lid had been forced open and when the Bill panted up, Harold was able to point the finger literally at the squat man and his mates and, with a composure that would have been remarkable in anyone but himself, was able to get across the salient points of the case. The Bill, of course, went crazy with joy over a fortuitously solved case.

Mr Blundy didn't die at once. When the Bill found him in the shattered Granada, upended on the safety barrier, he was able to speak.

"Get the kid out," he said painfully. "The little kid . . . car what hit me."

"All right, mate, just take it easy. Kid's all right."

Mr Blundy's fading eye focused on the Bill, a truly wonderful thing to see as one's last glimpse of earth. He knew he was a goner, knew it for sure: God had come back in that moment of crunch and crash and was even now manifesting Himself on the safety barrier and looking kind and welcoming. Mr Blundy had been good and had overcome the evil that had been resident in his spirit. Poor Ag: she'd carry the can on her own now; maybe already getting a lift down the M1, a lift into real trouble . . .

Mr Blundy heard someone say there were ambulances on the way.

He said faintly, "Want to see the kid, I do."

The Bill looked up and spoke to someone, sounding very far away now, and all at once it seemed Harold was there, white and shaky and wrapped in blankets, carried by the Bill. Mr Blundy murmured, "Sorry, son."

"Don't apologise. You've been awf'lly good really. I'm free now. You've been awf'lly decent . . . Mr Blundy."

Mr Blundy. Not just Blundy. That was really nice. "No hard feelings then, son?"

"None at all." There was a smile on the kid's face, Mr Blundy saw, but there were tears as well, and a very wobbly mouth. "Silly of you . . . trying to be Ayrton Senna."

"Sod Ayrton Senna, Nigel Mansell . . . little blighter."

Unable to say more, Harold just nodded. Mr Blundy, knowing it was all a joke, a friendly way of saying goodbye, gave a weak smile. Harold faded, so did the Bill, so did the motorway, all except the safety barrier, the Armco barrier like at Brands, and God sitting on it, plain as day and still smiling, still kind. Things were going to be okay and Mr Blundy felt warm and sort of sleepy, the pain fading as God's image grew. Just before he died he said with remarkable clarity, "Reckon He'd best hurry me through or He'll get cramp like as not."

"Who will?" the voice of the Bill asked.

"Up on the barrier. Can't you see Him?"

"No one on the barrier, mate," the Bill said.